MARIA

at the ec

MARIA PEURA

at the edge of light

Translated from the Finnish by

David Hackston

MAIA

Published in 2007 by
The Maia Press Limited
82 Forest Road
London E8 3BH
www.maiapress.com

First published in Finnish as *Valon reunalla*
by Teos in 2005

ISBN 978 1 904559 24 5

A CIP catalogue record for this book is available from
the British Library

Printed and bound in Great Britain

The Maia Press is indebted to Arts Council England
and FILI for financial support

River

Don't go on the ice, they said, they always said. The ice could break, shatter, you could fall through and drown. They always said that, and that's why you had to go. There was nowhere else. That safe, smooth surface. Skates slashed across the ice leaving jagged wounds that dripped with cold, blue blood. It felt good to touch it with your tongue, to know that death was near, within reach; your tongue didn't stick fast, the ice didn't tear it, didn't peel it like the hot sausages grilled for all the village to eat when the ice finally began to retreat. The spring sun was warm, though nature was still fast asleep. It would be months before the trees stuck out their green tongues and the earth deigned to let the flowers bud.

It would be months before anyone dared pack their winter coats away on the top shelf of the clothes cupboard and remove the raccoon-skin hats from their heads.

Anybody could peer in, read their terrifying thoughts and sneer:

'Daft girl, just like her father.'

Then they'd simper politely at Dad, his mouth caked in mustard and grease, grimace an attempted smile and say:

'Morning, Councillor. The ice'll crack soon, eh?'

I didn't say what I should have said. I didn't, though the ice was telling me to say it. Because the ice knew me. The river flowed through me, *me*; their rules didn't touch me. Don't go on the ice during the thaw.

I did go on the ice, though afterwards I was made to crouch over the edge of the bathtub and take the stinging swipes of the willow branches. I cried, the ice cried too, spring was far away and snow still lay hard and jagged on the shoulders of the willow trees. They leaned humbly towards the ice. The next time I escaped and ran out on to the ice, I crawled beneath the trees into an icy tunnel, wriggling against the hardened snow.

It was a greedy river. Come the spring floods it always swallowed someone up. One year a schoolgirl disappeared, bike, satchel, everything. Another year it gulped down two little twin boys. But more than any other year, people still talk about the time when the river went wild and swept away the old people's home. The whole village mucked in, gathering the old folk off floating blocks of ice. Those whom the river's black jaws had swallowed whole were still being dredged up that autumn. The river was greedy, it wanted to keep its prey. Sometimes it would cast a body on to a far-away shore, somewhere no one would think to look for it. Perhaps it took pleasure in being able to surprise a lonely fisherman with a decomposing human catch.

I never fell for its traps. I knew the river's mind, and I could tell when the ice started to move. Even as I dreamt, I could hear the first great crack tear open like thunder, and I knew how to choose the right routes. I didn't tumble into the deadly hole, though it was waiting, it had marked me with kisses and was waiting for me to give in and answer its call.

It called to me. It loved me. That's why I dared to resist it. Those the river did not call jumped blind and desperate to their deaths, expecting someone to reach out a warm hand at the last minute. The cemetery was full of people who had committed suicide. Amongst them were Grandpa and Uncle Eino. Mum told me what had happened years ago, but all I can remember is the smell of pine, the frosted wreaths laid on the coffin, the tears frozen to Mum's cheeks.

When my soul flew down it was spring too. The roads were under water and the railway line wasn't finished yet. No one ever came to visit the village, let alone live there. Children were born all the same, and I was one of them. I arrived like a gentle breeze, and only twelve years later did the end finally begin, the black veils descending on my soul, the raging hurricane that changed both me and the village.

During the war the village had been burnt to the ground, but they'd forgotten about Ruuhijärvi. There wasn't a proper road back then and the soldiers were in a hurry. They didn't have time to get lost in the middle of nowhere. That's why the old cabin still stands outside Grandma's house with my uncle's sleeping berth above the stove.

Dad restored the old family house by the riverside. By the time we moved in, my thoughts had turned from images into words. I was able to say.

'I'm Kristina, and one day I'm going to die too.'

My veins pulsed with strong blood, making my cheeks glow. Blood flowed through my mind, splitting it in two.

The river flowed through the village. There was the Finnish side and there was the Swedish side. On the Swedish side the boys were cocky, smiled so that their teeth showed, and wore only thin denim jackets during the winter. The girls wore thin jumpers with no bra and their nipples showed through. At Lennart's shop even children were allowed to buy chewing tobacco and light beer. On the Swedish side people laughed for no reason and there weren't enough deaths to warrant having their own cemetery. Of course, old folk passed away every now and then, dropped down dead in the middle of the afternoon, and they were then driven down to the rich soil of Matarenki. On the Swedish side, the crazy side, people drank home-brew at funerals and didn't quite know how to grieve. At the checkpoint, the customs officers winked lecherously and let you go through. On the healthy side, the Finnish side, you normally had to pull into the red lane, empty your pockets and open up your boot for the neighbours. Sometimes you'd have too much flour, sometimes margarine. You didn't get fined if you offered the customs officers a decent tipple. Spirits thawed their icy gaze.

On the Finnish side you didn't waste energy having fun. People worked hard, rebuilt the village, built houses of wood and brick, creating a village centre so that you could drive round and round. On the Swedish side all they could do was tear up and down along the same stretch of road. On a Saturday night the cocky Swedish boys would come across to the Finnish side, drive their Volvos in a circle around the village and park at midnight outside Hemppa's Caff. Their cars would soon be full of Finnish girls, then they'd drive off, to Kolari or Enontekiö, sometimes even up to the Arctic Sea. They drove for the joy of driving, and nobody ever asked after them, at least not on the Swedish side. On the Finnish side a police patrol would go out looking for you if your little escapade lasted too long.

Back home the girls would have the belt taken to them, but the next morning they would be smiling again, and come the weekend they'd be back loitering restlessly outside Hemppa's Caff. Hemppa gave out cigarettes on credit. He'd write the names of his debtors on a box of matches and stick it in his pocket. Anyone who agreed to stick their hand into Hemppa's pocket and wiggle it around had their debts forgiven.

I got neither forgiveness nor the belt. Mum and Dad were kind at heart. They stuck to willow branches and never hit hard. They believed in humiliation, not pain, in the quiet lamentation of the fragile skin. They believed in silence, a silence that couldn't be scoured from my lips with soap.

They believed in me.

I didn't get into the Volvo. Instead I walked down to the railway. I took off my mittens and stroked the tracks until my hand was frozen and the tracks were molten, and I could feel the shudder of the train in my chest. The temperature dropped another few degrees. With a great clap of thunder a new crack ripped through the thick ice and my heart counted the seconds.

Mansi

Aunt Mansi usually turned up in the summer. Her arrival never bode well. She wandered along the riverside and through the fields spreading out to the south of our house where the hay stretched peacefully up towards the sky.

And she cried.

Doors and windows locked themselves tight, and roller blinds lowered behind the windows. Mum and Dad forgot about the resentment they bore for one another and gathered around the table to curse in unison.

'She's got a cheek. A grown woman!'

'Wish she'd stay at home.'

'Barging into other folk's houses.'

'Pricey houses, too.'

I snuck a look out through the curtains. Mansi was leaning against the wall of a grey log barn, bawling. The neighbours had all gathered on the yard.

'She should be ashamed of herself,' yelled Mum.

Dad was more restrained. You don't badmouth your

relatives, at least not your own sister, her eyes swollen and twisted with grief. Eyes that stared at the landscape Dad had bought himself while his sister had been laid up in hospital.

Aunt Mansi had an inflammation of the ovaries. She had neither children nor a childhood home. She blamed Dad. He took the accusations, but still the front door remained shut. Aunt Mansi wasn't allowed inside. Dad hunched his shoulders and Mum talked without stopping for breath.

I opened and closed the blinds. They clung to my mind like glue. The movement stopped, my head throbbed. She should be ashamed. Ashamed. After Mansi left I waited for news of her death. Sometimes bells would start ringing before news reached us. An obituary was always happy news. It moved through the rooms in the house and lifted the rugs up from layers of collected dust. The wind blurred their appearances, dust settled in our lungs. Bad news, Mum kept repeating in a stifled voice until I finally believed her.

'When you're young you think life will go on forever, but just you wait.'

I breathed Mansi into my lungs.

Then the train rolled into the village and delivered a coffin in which she lay in pieces, and nobody dared look inside.

The same route had been taken by those before her. The freight train to Kemi, then change. The corridors were narrow on the train of death. There was no room for her to walk along and she fell out. Nobody knew why, or whether someone had pushed her or whether she had jumped. Nobody knew, and that's why they didn't cry at the funeral. Crying wasn't appropriate, as there was always the chance that she might have jumped. It wasn't appropriate. And without permission, too.

Mansi was crazy.

With a tingling sense of compulsion I set off in Mansi's footsteps. I walked alongside the tracks. That's where life began, if only you dared to die first. I was the one to decide when to sever the thread connecting the soul to the body, just as the umbilical cord had once connected me to Mum. Everyone had the power to decide for themselves. Mansi knew this best of all. She knew that not everyone can cope with being enveloped in the prolonged dusk which forces you to walk down the steps and settle on the damp floor in the basement. Mansi knew the panic which makes your limbs convulse in the grip of uninvited dreams. She knew that there were two kinds of suiciders. Those who escape as winter lays down its black shroud, and those who disappear with the shadows, as someone unexpectedly switches the lights on.

I was captivated by the lights which hid amongst those black cloaks, lighting the winter darkness with a mysterious glow. Spring light didn't shock me, but added to the restlessness which commanded me to run away, to the train tracks, towards that merciful noise that killed all other thoughts.

Flats

It's hard to resist the forbidden. The house stood by the riverside and the ice was close. The ice spoke, forcing me onwards. The ice was strong and able to carry me. You reached the village quicker if you walked along the ice. From the riverbank you could sneak across to the forbidden flats.

The flats were full of drunks and mental folk. That's why we weren't allowed to go there. Maaru lived there too. And Nina. And Kari. Their clothes stank of smoke and grease. Because of them we had to air the classroom, even in the middle of winter. Because of the flats everyone in school froze.

The flats were responsible for Grandpa's death too. Beneath the ice the water flowed towards the flats, a mighty current. Grandpa, who usually always skied down to the petrol station for a drink, had skied to the flats instead. His skis stood propped against the grey stone wall as he walked up to the fourth floor, stepped into the room, stopped by the bed and saw a woman lying there; inside her lay another man, while inside Grandpa there was no one. Now he is no longer there, because he strode out to the balcony, climbed on to the railing and toppled backwards. His head split open on the frozen earth, and naturally they didn't have an open casket at the funeral, though it was an ancient village tradition.

'Your Grandpa was good man. Skied a lot,' Mum sighed.

Kari told a different story. His mother knew what happened. His mother, Raakel, had been huddling beneath the bed when Grandpa walked into the room. Back then Raakel didn't have dark bags beneath her eyes or a saggy stomach. Back then she had bright, sparkling eyes which saw everything from beneath the bed.

At school Kari drank copying fluid and kicked the overhead projector to pieces. They dragged him along the school corridors by the scruff of the neck and locked him in a small room where a special needs teacher examined him from behind her thick spectacles.

'Retarded, abnormal,' the teacher wrote in her papers, and Kari threw up in the waste-paper bin.

Nobody inspected Kari's internal organs. They were left to rot in peace. His wicked gaze bored its way through the walls into the gym and shot poisoned arrows into my legs as I was trying to obey the teacher's instructions.

'One and two and one and two and . . . Faster, Kristina!' bellowed the teacher and straightened her pleated gym skirt.

I tripped over and she pointed to the stage.

'Show the others how. And one and two and one and two . . . !'

I spread my legs and something appeared. Strange and repugnant, making my limbs twitch when I was sitting still. It appeared and jumped out of me; for a moment I danced with it and I could feel how my body moved effortlessly. This goddess of my contortions wasn't wearing a dark-red gypsy skirt. She was ugly and formless. The corners of her mouth drooped downwards. Her eyes gazed emptily in different directions. She kept her distance when I smiled at her. When I gave her a stern look she disappeared back inside me, and I couldn't ask for forgiveness because I could no longer see her.

And with that we marched into the showers. The water was icy and my skin was covered in goose pimples, and the teacher stood in the doorway, fully dressed, bellowing:

'Armpits and backside, armpits and backside!'

Amid fits of giggles I poked at my armpits and lost my rhythm. The teacher clapped her hands together faster and faster. At break-time my wet hair instantly turned to icicles that I could stick in Maaru's mouth.

'My teeth'll freeze,' she howled.

Nobody came to help her. Maaru was a commie. She went to the Pioneers club in Kittisvaara, and if the weather was really cold they'd drive her to school in their battered old Moskvitch.

'Commie junk, commie junk,' we sang in chorus as Maaru whimpered in the middle of the bully circle.

Onni sang the loudest of all, so that nobody would remember that his parents owned a Lada. I remembered. I let him sing in peace, until I suddenly shoved Maaru into the snow and turned my wicked eyes on Onni.

'Ladas are good cars for the winter,' he whispered, but nothing could save him now.

We pushed him to the far end of the playground and locked him in the special needs toilets. Then the bell rang and my armour crumbled. Fear spilled on to my chest, and before it had frozen one of the special needs kids had toppled me to the ground and rubbed my face in the hard snow and shoved snow down my neck.

I sat alone in the playground, my mouth full of snow water, wishing that Mum would come and carry me home, gently rub stinging ointment on my face and dab it with cotton wool until everything shrank, evaporated, disappeared, that strange, repugnant thing that appeared when I was walking, sitting, sleeping, lying awake, waiting for Kari to be let out of the special needs teacher's tomb. I would close my goddess inside Mum's tender fist, and purify myself with the smell of vanilla. Dad would take us both in the palm of his hand, and Mum wouldn't fear him.

Dad was a dark giant who collapsed on Mum, but she was too tired to push him away. She would rather stagger towards the greyness that was approaching our house as it stood there, every entrance wide open.

Kari

Kari had fox's eyes. When the noise in his head was too loud, his eyes narrowed into thin slits and a bloody wound opened up in his lower lip. It fascinated me. In my dreams I pressed my lips against his and sucked until his gaunt face was white and bloodless. I dared look him in the eye when we bumped into each other in the shop doorway. He had stolen two packets of cigarettes. Beneath my coat I hid three lipsticks and a porn magazine.

'Want to swap?' asked Kari with a flick of the head. His hair streamed down across his face. It was animal-coloured and gave off a red glow that caught in my face too.

'No thanks,' I said and pulled my cap down over my eyes.

Kari disappeared into the darkness. Beneath my shirt the magazine had become slippery with sweat. Outside it turned to ice along which Kari would skate towards me as the brightly coloured night arrived once again. His shadow was longer than those of the spruces in the yard. His smile was resplendent, dispelling the grey.

His smile died away whenever someone mentioned Pekka. Kari's cousin Pekka had hitched a lift to Kemi where he had boarded the train of death. He wandered along those narrow corridors, but the door didn't suck him out. He wandered all night long and only died the following morning; in Helsinki, on the tram tracks. He stood firmly on the tracks and wouldn't move, no matter how much the driver tooted the horn. It ran in their family, that kind of persistence. Kari was proud of him. He wouldn't have moved either. No one could have forced him.

Kari never tired of telling this story. He came out into the yard and crashed his scooter into the verge of snow, and he didn't shut his mouth, not even when his father ran outside and hurled him against the verge. His mouth chewed the snow until it melted, allowing the swear words to pass his lips again. That was why I loved him. There was power in those words, a power that flowed into me too, even though Dad dragged me home by the scruff of the neck and locked the door.

Waiting was pointless. Pekka wasn't going to come back from the dead to tell us why he had never finished his journey; why, even after death, he still clenched his fist around a scrap of paper with an address. He never told us where he was going when death finally tripped him up. He never spoke to us, though we were on his side and the rest of the village was against him.

The village despised all those who left. They hated us too, though we were still only planning our final escape.

We used to escape the village. We would hide from its gaze in the forest or the cemetery where the gravestones were so close together that there was no room for the trees to grow. We knew why the freight train brought the village so many dead and so few living. It was the village's fault. It had a wicked soul. The grown-ups didn't know this. We knew, but no one asked us. Death was within us; it was alive. Asking would have been too dangerous.

We both worshipped Pekka, who was finally laid to rest next to Mansi. We worshipped Erkki too, when he soon afterwards lay down to sleep next to his brother. It was almost a rule. When one person died, someone else would soon follow suit, someone from the same family. Erkki and Pekka were brothers. Erkki left for Helsinki to see where Pekka had died, but he never made it. He stood too close to a door that the conductor had left open and the wind wrenched him out of the carriage.

On the backs of the headstones we carved our own marks with the end of a knife. We blew out the candles laid at the graves of suiciders. We worshipped them in the dark and no new candles were ever brought to their graves. The parents of those who died so young drove south. They were looking for stations with real waiting rooms and staff who made announcements. They sat on the hard benches waiting, waiting for the trains to come, at the right time; hoping the years wouldn't wreak havoc after all, hoping they'd roll slowly back along the tracks, to brighten as they approached the village, giving life once again to their children. And everything could start over.

At the village station stood piles of logs and a small, flat-roofed cottage where the railway workers brewed coffee and liquor. Its doors were always locked fast. No one made announcements. The freight train arrived twice a day. It stopped in the village, unloaded or took on more cargo, then continued north to Kolari. The tracks didn't go any further than that. That's where the world ended and the passenger train was still far away, months away from the village.

Kari took out his knife and pressed its blunt edge against my neck.

'Don't be afraid,' he whispered.

I swallowed my fear and listened to the thinning hiss as Kari drew the edge of the knife along my skin. He cured me the way the ancient Lapps have done for centuries. He didn't pierce the skin; he merely scratched the points that felt ill.

There wasn't a single point within me that didn't care for Kari's touch. A rusty knife was better than him leaving me. He didn't leave me. I took off my shoes and showed him my bare feet. He didn't ask anything, didn't look me in the eyes, but he knew that the nerves reaching to the heart lie in the soles of our feet. He spat out a gob of chewing tobacco, followed its black trajectory through the air and pressed the knife hard into my foot.

I couldn't escape him any longer. He found me, followed my blood trail, even once the wound had healed. Once he had caught the scent, he couldn't forget, so he said. In that respect he was like his father. His father had only left Raakel alone after being forcibly removed. And once he'd served his sentence, he'd be back. So he had sworn.

Kari swore on his father's name. I tried not to laugh in his face. I knew what fathers were like. I'd seen one close up and a few others from a distance. I knew what fathers were like. I knew that they couldn't be trusted. Kari only believed in his father because he wasn't there.

The knife was real. Its blade was rusted, but it was real. No sooner had its tip brushed against those tender islands of pain than I was healed. I was healed when I saw Kari's mischievous smile, compelling me to take off my jacket and jumper, to reveal my skin and what lay beneath my skin; that made goose pimples appear on the surface, so clamorous that I had to stuff my ears with moss. The noise came from within. Nobody heard it but me. Not even Kari, though I told him to press his ear against my skin. All he heard was my heartbeats, and he counted them out loud. He counted them until they slowed, leaving space for something new, and the noise no longer fitted inside me.

It moved into Kari, without a sound.

Noise without sound is like an itch. Itching is a cunning form of pain.

Kari said it was the devil scratching. It would come while Kari was asleep, and always started on his back. The worst of the thrashing had been when Kari was just a baby and his father had still lived at home. So Raakel had said. Sometimes they had to cancel appointments at the clinic because the skin on his back had all but disappeared.

Kari was scared of the devil. The devil would take him by the hand and lead him. During the daytime Kari would bite his nails to the quick and straighten the edges with a knife. And still by morning his skin would be covered in blood. Every morning. This is how he knew it must have been the devil. A devil with very long nails.

It was hard to talk; the devil was so close to him, so firmly pressed against him, one of its limbs constantly inside him. And sometimes it would wedge its eyes in behind Kari's eyes and look at me, and it frightened me, but Kari never understood why I turned away and refused to kiss him.

'Fucking dog,' he would shout.

From the tone of his voice I knew that the devil had puckered his lips into a trumpet and forced them in behind

Kari's lips, and that if I didn't run away fast they would spit at me, like the third time we met; like last month; like the day before yesterday. Never again. My clothes were stained and Mum was furious. The devil's spit was black and sticky. It caught in my face like phlegm. Mum would look at me in disgust and at school I'd be asked to leave the room.

Not that Kari would be standing in the corridor to console me. He had already been sent away; away from the big brick school to a small wooden school with only a few pupils in each class and where the teacher had more time for them. The wooden school was in Lempeä, a meek little village far away from the flats, and social services even gave Kari tickets for the bus. Then Raakel came up with the idea of taking the tickets away, selling them and using the money to buy beer. And so Kari had to run to school. He ran along the side of the road, but it was a long way and school had finished by the time he got there. His teacher approached him in the doorway and said:

'Shame on you.'

After that he ran along the train tracks. He ran in front of the train and got to school in time and his teacher said nothing. Not even when he arrived at school with his toes frozen. His teacher had been leaning towards the blackboard writing out the seven times table in a shaky, faltering hand when Kari took off his shoes and tapped his frozen toes against the floor. Later on, one of them had to be amputated. Only one toe. Kari should be grateful, his teacher said, an old man who often nodded off mid-sentence. Sometimes his sentences were very long indeed. The bell would ring for break and the teacher would carry on sleeping, and no one knew whether to wait for him to wake up or slip outside and sway with the trees until the bell rang again, instructing them to swap the mathematics books for R.E. You couldn't wake him up, never ever, because then the teacher had become someone else, someone from his dream, someone who picked up the cane and lashed out. Not carefully, on the fingers, like they did back in the brick school, but thrashing around at random. The cane struck whoever happened to be in the way, and only once the teacher had properly awoken did he put down his cane and continue talking in his normal voice, almost as if he was unaware he'd been lashing out. He was a meek man. The village had even been named after him. His father had been meek too and all their fathers before them. And God was meek. In R.E. classes the teacher always remembered to mention this. God was meek and for that we should all be thankful, particularly Kari who had only lost one toe out of ten. One big toe. In its absence he walked a bit awkwardly, rocking like a camel.

Armas

They say that suiciders are condemned to repeat their violent deeds for all eternity. Behind them they leave guilt and shame. People either talk about them in shameful whispers or hold their silence altogether, not realising that the dead see everything and hear everything. Some people die peacefully and calmly continue their journey. The minds of those who die a violent death are restless and confused. They easily latch on to morbid thoughts and remain near the body, going round and round in an agonised circle. Once the spirit is frozen in restless motion, the cause of death no longer matters. What's important is to foster sympathy for the deceased and allow them to continue their journey.

I can't remember my birth, and I can't remember the years immediately afterwards, but my body certainly remembers. My body still bears the marks of my unsuccessful attempts at breathing. My throat remembers the throttling, my chest the suffocating. Mum couldn't sleep because I made strange noises. I breathed in too much air at once and couldn't breathe it out without spluttering. While holding my breath I coughed and wheezed, and every now and then my face would turn blue and my body fall limp. The very moment I was born I began dying, but they never did build a coffin for me.

They built it for Armas instead.

Armas hanged himself from one of the fence posts. I discovered him.

Armas lived with Nadja in a house nearby. They owned a shiny, black racehorse that I used to take care of. I'd sometimes find Armas asleep in one of the stalls and drag him back to the cottage. Horse manure fell from his clothes on to their beautiful rugs, but Nadja just laughed. She was terminally ill and no longer had the strength to care. Nor did she have the strength to undress before lying down on the pull-out bed. I stared at her layers of skirts and her sparkling earrings until she told me to leave.

'Your Mammy won't like you hanging about here.'

She was right. Mum didn't like it. Nobody in the village liked the gypsies, especially not unruly ones like Nadja and Armas. They had moved into the village against the will of their people, and not even the death sentence could make them move away again. They lived in its shadow. They lived in peace until Nadja fell ill and died and Armas killed himself.

I didn't touch him. I ran into the stable and stroked the horse as it lay on the ground, until my hand turned red and I realised that it had died too.

'Murder-suicide,' said Dad, matter-of-fact.

I rinsed my eyes and soon I no longer remembered.

Dad struck his name from the petition to force Nadja and Armas out of the village. Then he built a coffin and started making arrangements for the funeral.

The horse wasn't buried. It rotted away in the stable, until the stable was burned down. Walking past their deserted house, I always thought I could hear the sound of neighing. Even if I took a different route I could hear it. When the house was burned and a new one built of brick in its place, the neighing stopped. No gypsies moved into the village after that. It felt empty, lonely.

Crow

'Our Bible,' said Kari and handed me the book.

I opened it to keep him happy. I shut it when he threw himself on the ground and closed his eyes. The black Bible. I'd read it before. I'd read everything else that I found in the library too. In his whole life Kari had never read anything else. As the hurricane drew closer, I allowed myself not to read it.

I allowed myself to take the form of a crow and fly above the fields. I allowed myself to emerge from my body and fly further than the crows, letting my weightless mind assume the form of an eagle and soar above the clouds.

When I returned, I was heavy, the taste of metal and mouldy hay in my mouth. Still, there was always a good reason to undertake that journey. I knew what death was, and I wasn't afraid. I wasn't afraid of the train. Walking along the tracks I would slow my steps as the train hurtled forwards, while the others started to run. I refreshed myself in the waters of death, knowing that the final transition was yet to come. As I let go I had already seen my burial mound, my name chiselled into the gravestone, the cross before my final day. I knew that no one would come to collect me for a long time, and that if they did, I would have nothing to be afraid of. I would be weightless, anybody, anything; a leaf bobbing in the wind, sap racing up the insides of the tree trunks. I would be alive in some form. I wouldn't be that body, those walls, those shells.

That's why I had the courage to flirt with pain and death. I don't know who started it. It was wonderful to yank hairs from my head and examine their roots. Beneath the skin was a whole world pulsating in the wrong direction. No eyes could see the slow movement of its tissues, no ears hear the soft squelching of its internal organs. You had to take a knife, set the blade against the skin and push until the shell opened up and revealed its secrets.

'Cut lengthways, then you'll die for sure,' Kari advised me.

The hand holding the knife felt suddenly heavy.

'I can't.'

'Can't do nothing, you,' he agreed.

My hand pressed the knife deeper.

'Your Grandpa would've had the guts.'

Wincing with pain, I put the finishing touches to our initials and handed the knife back to Kari. He didn't have the guts. I let the knife fall to the ground and moved closer.

Pain swallowed up the years. I was young, shouting for Grandpa, but he was already on the roof. He keeled backwards and slumped against the tarmac . . . but this time he stood up, walked back up the stairs and on to the roof and jumped again and again and again. The sun sprang up from behind a cloud and melted the tarmac; Grandpa thumped down into a soft pit and didn't die after all. He stood up, scratched his head and started walking towards the house, towards the reindeer fences which, instead of lying rotting beneath the house, now stood upright and pushed the house away. Grandpa walked right through the fences in the direction of Ruuhijärvi. To this day he is still travelling, with Uncle walking behind him. Uncle never stops walking. Death can never stop their journey.

Kari walked along the train tracks from the school in Lempeä, where they had sent him to calm down. I waited for him behind the special needs building. I drew a bitter toke on a cigarette stub and didn't dare go back to school, though I sprayed my clothes, hair and mouth with deodorant. The teacher had a keen sense of smell and could smell the burnt reek on me even when I hadn't been smoking.

'Cut lengthways,' Kari insisted.

He didn't really wish me to die. He was just sulking because I didn't dare follow him to the flats, where Grandpa's outline haunted the yard and the stink of fried grease hung like a thick wall in the stairwell. Kari carried the knife to cut through that wall. He came home, but never to his mother. Raakel spent the daytime mopping floors at the hospital and the nights bagging breadcrumbs at the bakery. It was just the two of them. As for his father, Kari wasn't really sure.

Kari's father's outline in the tarmac was fainter than Grandpa's. His father had shot himself in the head, but the path the bullet had chosen meant that he didn't die, he was only disabled from the waist down. Kari never got a little brother, though they had planned for one. His father wheeled himself out of the village in his wheelchair and put his gun to someone else's forehead. This time the bullet chose a fatal path and he landed up in the county prison in Oulu. Raakel burned every photograph and Kari soon forgot what his father looked like, though the violet ovals his father had pressed into Raakel's face with the hot iron wouldn't go no matter how much she scrubbed. Now every time he saw his mother, Kari saw those scars and thought: Dad. She would often disappear for several days at a time, allowing Kari to forget everything for a brief moment.

Raakel never married again, though she went out with men on the nights when someone else was bagging bread-crumbs for her. Gradually Kari's fear turned into an X-ray vision that meant he could see everything that went on in his mother's bedroom. Through the sweaty skin he could see her internal organs, and through the organs he could see into the neighbouring flats where even at night nobody went to sleep. Like Raakel years ago, the children hid beneath their beds and only scrambled under the blankets once the last of the adults had passed out. It could even have been morning by then, and Kari's eyes bored through the outer walls and wandered around the village until they hit upon a house, a kitchen, a beautifully laid table, children still drunk with sleep sitting there talking to their parents before it was time to leave for school.

This was my house. Or so he said. I allowed him this fantasy. I hadn't dared take him inside my home, and in his fantasy it had become a palace, a place where he had no business except maybe as a stable boy for the horses that had died years ago. It was such a horrible thought that you had to laugh out loud.

Kari got cross and told me yet again to cut lengthways. I picked up the knife, placed the blade against the fine skin on my forearm and pressed.

'You're a daft lass,' he said tenderly as the black blood began to flow.

Dinner

In Mum's arctic world food was dry and fat-free. Dad made it through the winters by hoarding cupboards full of beer and cheap salami. Mum looked with disgust at the flabby mountain slowly growing around Dad's heart.

'Eating for two, I see.'

'You talking to me or her?' Dad sneered and gave me a wink.

I heaped a mountain of rice on to my plate and doused it in gravy. It was Sunday. On Sundays Mum turned a blind eye and the gravy was good, creamy. I poured it straight into my mouth. Mum carved the roast and didn't say a thing. I ate a plateful, a second, a third, and although the rice was polished and white it swelled in my stomach and forced me to slump beneath the table.

Dad exploded with laughter.

'You can't half eat, lass!'

Mum laid the table again and I crawled back to my place.

For pudding there was apple pie with vanilla sauce.

Dad didn't want any. He was saving room for more drinks, first wine, then beer, then cognac. Mum didn't want any either, so I took a great big chunk. I gulped it down without chewing. It tasted of the rice which was still trying to force its way back up towards my throat. Mum popped a round little pill into her mouth and swallowed it with a swig of tap water.

Dad raised his glass. His face was ruddy and contented. Mum's vanilla cheeks glowed, joy glistening in her eyes. I tried to steal just a little piece of it for myself, but my chair disappeared from beneath me and the world turned upside down.

Dad had cut a hole in the ice into which I sunk my aching stomach. The current in the river was particularly strong near our house. During the summer you couldn't jump off the bank for a swim, but now I was able to submit myself to the river and let its icy waters numb my body. I wanted to dive down under the ice and swim with the undercurrent, which I thought would grow warmer downstream, but even a few minutes under water began to crush my lungs. The icy waters compressed my thoughts to a cold stone and I had to come up to the surface and follow Dad's footprints back up to the house, through the back door and straight into the sauna.

Mum stood wrapped in a towel, shivering in the doorway, and sneered at Dad as he whooped and wriggled about in the soft banks of snow.

My pain had remained in the water. I bobbed in the warmth of the frozen current, naked and proud, and let the wind make every hair on my skin stand on end. How happy I felt as I sat between Mum and Dad in the dim light of the sauna, soaking up the acrid smell of tar. Dad's skin was slippery with sweat as he reached out his hand to throw more water on the stove.

Mum hummed a melody as she combed my wet hair; I had grown up to the melancholy strains of that music. I nestled against her. The plaintive quiver of her voice foreshadowed the days, weeks, months she was to spend lying in the darkened bedroom in her nightdress. The song tells of a woman waiting for her husband. The days go by. Men in soldiers' uniforms arrive at the neighbouring houses. Weeping, celebration, shots fired in jubilation. Sunday comes and the woman looks out of the window. A coffin is carried in through the gate.

Hundreds of people had committed suicide upon hearing this song.

Mum had hummed away while I rocked in the ocean of her womb. She was still humming when I began to follow her around. I tried to convince myself that Mum had no reason to kill herself. Dad wasn't away at war, and he always returned from his various odysseys in time for Sunday dinner. Mum wouldn't kill herself. I repeated this to myself out loud, over and over, the time she stopped breathing after swallowing a handful of painkillers and I had to stick my fingers down her throat.

'Music is the best medicine of all,' she said once she'd woken up, and shuffled over to the piano.

Gloomy is Sunday, with shadows I spend it all.
My heart and I have decided to end it all.
Soon there'll be candles and prayers that are sad I know.
Let them not weep, let them know that I'm glad to go.
Death is no dream for in death I'm caressing you;
With the last breath of my soul I'll be blessing you.
Gloomy Sunday.

Mum's voice shook the house's foundations. The spirit of the river swirled in through the windows. When Dad wanted to row out into the river and fish for orange-laced perch, I calmed its waves. You had to appease the river until the winter cold froze it, shackled its will and allowed people to drive their augers deep into its fragile heart.

I too sat there ice-fishing. I leant my cheek against the softness of Dad's lambskin coat and felt a tightening in my mouth; the river felt it too, as the cold compressed the water's memory and forced it to remain solid through the long winter. I clenched my teeth and wished for spring to come, for the sun to caress the covering of ice until it became brittle. The river's true surface lay beneath that thin crust of ice, and in the summer, when the ice seemed to have melted entirely, you could see a clear film stretching across the surface of the water: the river's gentle, glistening aura.

Few people knew that you had to tread on the river's surface as you would through the forest: cautiously, and with respect. You had to stand on the shore for a long time, allow thoughts to come and go until they were no more than gossamer clouds in the sky. You had to let the light appear and illuminate the river, so that it might silently respond:

'Come!'

But few ever heard a response.

If I obeyed the river, it would protect me. Otherwise it would grind its teeth as I walked along its skin, let out hollow sighs and suddenly open before me a pitch-dark crack, through which the bluish limbs of those drowned in the spring floods reached upwards. I could be next. I had learned to dive down until darkness engulfed my mind and I became light and graceful as a fish. I learned to wait for the jingling of bells and the arrival of angels radiating brilliant light through their underwater kingdom, and only then would I swim to the surface and allow the waves to carry me ashore on a faraway island.

Doughnut

The dog was greedy. That's why we called him Doughnut. Doughnut had long curly ears. His lips sagged towards the floor. Whenever we sat down at the dinner table a trail of slobber would drip from his muzzle. A puddle soon appeared on the floor, reflecting the sadness in Doughnut's eyes when his bowl wasn't refilled.

'Only morning and evening,' Mum insisted.

When Mum retired to her bedroom I filled the bowl so much that Doughnut threw up.

He was my dog. I ran him up and down the village so that he wouldn't get fat. After overeating his movements were always a bit stiff.

'It'll eat itself to death, that dog,' warned Pirta.

I stroked Doughnut's shiny coat contentedly. 'Who's a brave boy?' I whispered in his ear.

'He's not interested. Anyway, just think of Anneli,' she said.

'What about her?'

'What d'you think?'

'Tried to top herself.'

'Right.'

Anneli lived in Kaukonen. She was Pirta's cousin, who would do just about anything. Shave her head with a beard trimmer, stick a hot needle through her earlobe, turn up at school drunk – even though her dad was a teacher there.

'Swallowed a tubful of contraceptives.'

'Of what?'

'You know, pills.'

'She didn't die then?'

'No, she didn't want to.'

Pirta twirled her finger through Doughnut's curls. Then she burst into tears.

'She's so alive it makes me sick,' she sobbed.

Kauko

The village was a labyrinth, and at the centre stood Hemppa's stinking Caff. It was almost unbearable to walk along those hallowed corridors wrapped in the burnt smell of deep-fried sausage and chips. If you took too long getting there the Swedish boys would already have gone, leaving only Kauko Hartikainen sitting in his red Fiat. The doors to Kauko's Fiat were open and the seats were still covered in their protective plastic. He didn't want the car getting mucky, didn't want anyone to spill booze on the velvet upholstery. Kauko was our driver. He would always drive us around if we asked him. He would drive slowly along the riverside, and you could see his roving eyes in the rear-view mirror. He watched us, making sure our cigarette ends didn't burn the plastic seat covers. He watched, checking to see which of us was already wearing a bra. If we were wearing too many clothes, he would turn the heating on full blast and wait for us to strip off. Sweat ran down his face, and sometimes he'd have to stop the car and go outside for a moment to cool off. He never came in the back seat though, he never even tried, and no one ever went and sat next to him in the passenger seat.

Once, when we weren't in the car, he drove off the road and died. They dragged him out of the written-off car and laid him in a coffin, but the Fiat remained in the woods. Little by little it rusted away.

We polished off any bottles in the boot that hadn't smashed. Slowly we got used to the idea that there was nobody to drive us around any more. We only got the occasional lift, and some of the drivers were dangerous, like the punks that came down from Äkäslompolo, rampaged through the village, then drove to the cemetery. Blood and booze began to flow and gravestones were toppled over. The police interviewed those who were still around the following Monday. I learned to be wary of the boys from Muonio after they offered me a swig of methanol. The boys from Ylitornio were arrogant; they kept their car doors locked and you never got a drop of anything out of them. The boys from Kemi talked funny and looked down their noses at us until they had their noses smashed in by one of the braver boys from our village, and after that the Kemi boys didn't dare enter the village unarmed. Shotguns and axes appeared in the rear windows of their cars. The police in Kittilä sat around drinking coffee and Hemppa no longer dared fry his hamburgers without a bullet-proof vest. We headed for the woods.

The village was a sun spreading its rays of light in all directions. At the end of each ray there was a cottage. In front of each cottage was a bare scrap of woodland garden, a sauna and a lake. Every lake had a different name, and no matter which lake we chose we could always get a lift there. Somebody's parent took us on Friday, somebody else's collected us on Sunday. They didn't want to know what exactly we got up during our stays at these cottages. They were glad to be able either to drink the weekend away in peace or get together to pray and speak in tongues.

No one kept an eye on us, and yet the woods were full of eyes. As it grew dark we pulled the curtains to and gathered in front of the fireplace to play. Drinking glasses slid across letters scribbled on a sheet of baking paper, and the fireplace devil spat out burning embers which, at the name of Jesus, went out before the fire could spread. A spirit moved through whichever remote village we had chosen and before long the cottage was full of the local boys. Pirta was mad about the boys from Rattosjärvi, their hair combed back with tar. I liked the way the boys from Juoksenki pulled faces and cracked their knuckles. The boys from Alposjärvi gnawed on dried meat like it was chewing gum and their breath smelled of sweaty socks. I never agreed to kiss them, especially once I had tasted Kari's sweet lips. I concentrated on emptying their stocks of spirits; they also varied greatly. Some of them offered us stuff they'd bought at the off-licence, others brought over-fermented mead or home-brew cloudy with yeast. Hangovers were always good, especially if you pressed your fists against your weary eyes and dared to look at the terrifying pictures reflected on the inside of your eyelids. Together we dared look at them.

In the sauna we would look at one another, though we only ever dared go in during the hours of daylight. You had to throw lots of water on the stove to make your growing nipples and flabby tummy disappear in clouds of steam. Sweating burned calories and lightened the load. It dissolved the guilt and stopped my heart for a moment if a painful thought wouldn't go away.

'And what did you get up to?' our parents asked on the journey home.

'We ran about the woods and sat in the sauna. In the evenings we played cards.'

'That's my girl.'

Our parents shined and polished their cars and houses, but they didn't care about their cottages. Cottages were supposed to be run-down. It didn't matter if the all the fabrics were thick with tobacco breath, as smoke from the fireplace smothered all other smells. Some people went and checked the cottage after we'd been there, closed the flue and made sure that the key was hidden under the right stone.

Annukka's dad was the worst. He brought his face up close whenever he asked how you were, and he could smell the petrol and the stink of old spirits even though our mouths were full of sweets. He could smell it even after we'd been chewing on frozen pine needles and brushed our teeth with pine-scented soap. Still, he never once told tales on us. He was even worse than Dad when it came to sleeping around and Annukka knew far too much about his dalliances. Annukka escaped into the attic whenever he beat her mum black and blue – everywhere but the face. In the village you had to keep your face clean. It was an essential part of staying alive. For Annukka's dad this required particular effort. As we drove back towards the village he would let the car veer out to the left and cruise at thirty for the whole journey, making absolutely sure that no one could overtake us. On the back seat we ducked down and tried to make ourselves invisible in case we happened to drive past one of our boyfriends.

If the cause of your humiliation was great enough, you could show no mercy, not even to your best friend. I learned to read from people's expressions when I'd be better off falling ill and missing school, so that I wouldn't end up in the bully circle.

As you grow up you learn to fine-tune your body. I sucked the thermometer until the mercury showed the right temperature. The reading couldn't be too high though. It was pointless being really ill if you wanted to enjoy any special treatment at home, swallow bitter antibiotics every time your windpipe became inflamed and savour the taste of the fizzy orange juice and milk chocolate that Dad had rushed out to buy. I controlled my fever with sheer will-power. Particularly satisfying was the time my appendix swelled up at my command and my stomach was cut open just as the pus was about to explode into my abdomen. Adults knelt before me and were forced to give me the one thing I most wanted: morphine! I returned to school triumphant. I was immune to scorn and insult until it was time for my check-up and the doctor stuck his finger in my vagina. There wasn't enough room. Nobody had ever been in there before. The bottom of my stomach filled with flames. My sutures burst open. I cried out loud, but the doctor just smiled.

'Try thinking of something else, think about the summer holidays!' he whispered as he stuck another finger in my anus.

The window was garlanded in frost flowers. Behind them the frosted eyes of my friends gazed at me. Defeat was branded on my face and in its red-hot glow the ice melted. Too eagerly. Too soon.

Uncle

Not even my uncle could predict things at first; not until he was seven, when he tried to save a litter of kittens which had been tied in a sack and thrown into the lake at Ruuhijärvi. My uncle dived in after them and struggled with the drawstring until the sack opened up and the kittens managed to get out. Their instinct took them ashore and back to the barn where their mother sat crying. Uncle sobbed himself full of water and sank to the bottom of the lake. By the time they found him he had stopped breathing. He only came round as the kittens were being drowned again. The spirits of those seven cats transmigrated into him. He became the youngest of all the village idiots, and his brain turned into a calculator. He remembered everything; he didn't know how to forget things. He wandered around, trying to escape his own thoughts. He didn't dare run, his ears seemed to be full of water, water from Ruuhijärvi, and the water was full of cats' piss. He walked faster and faster, but his calculations followed him everywhere. Anyone who walked past him soon learned exactly how many hours they had lived, what day of the week they were born and how closely their birth matched the first thawing of the ice that year.

As he slowed down, my uncle could feel time stopping and drawing a breath. Uncle breathed in too, but then time began running ahead of him, flashing symbols at him, and again he had to speed up and tell everyone what the future held in store, when the ice would melt. He predicted this to the day, the hour, the minute. Predicting the future eventually took its toll on Uncle. That's why he was put in care. Grandma mollycoddled him; she spooned porridge into his mouth until he threw up on his plate, then she'd burst into tears.

'What a waste! His life's just trickling away.'

Grandma never calmed down, not even when, quick as a flash, Uncle began listing how many spoonfuls of porridge he had managed to keep down this year and how many times he had pooped the porridge down the outdoor loo. Neither did she take comfort at the fact that as many days had passed since Grandpa's death as Grandma had years left to live. Grandma was a pious woman and couldn't abide such prophecies.

'I've been condemned to live with the Devil.'

And as she uttered the word *devil*, fear flashed across Uncle's eyes. It was a brilliant, burning bolt of lightning and Uncle yelped sharply. His ears began to ring. The sound was high-pitched and persistent. For a moment it drowned out the rattling of his calculator. Uncle's head was swimming, and he couldn't say when it would happen, when the ice would begin to complain, when the first crack would tear it open.

Hairs

A hurricane was blowing its way through Uncle's head. I had summoned it, through the pain, unbeknownst even to myself, though I was only twelve and wished that I could carry on dreaming deep, strong, milky dreams. I woke with a start as my womb began to contract and my pores opened up, pushing out hairs that were thick and rough as tree trunks. The soft down, which had protected my body from the time I was born, gave way and soon my arms and legs were covered in a black carpet of hair. Between my legs there appeared a pitch-black strip of hair that quickly sprouted into a dense jungle. My breasts swelled. The vegetation spread to my armpits too. I was changed in a single, stormy night that was duly crowned by the appearance of a couple of bulrushes jutting up from the dark skin around my nipples.

'You're like a monkey, lass,' Dad lamented.

'Yuck!' shouted Pirta.

Mum awoke from her slumber and handed me the razor. Pirta dragged me into the bathroom. She had received instructions on what to do from her penfriend in America. You lather your legs in shaving cream and shave until there's no cream or hair left. It sounded easy. I stood in the bathtub, humbled, wishing I could exchange bodies with Pirta. She was thin and hairless, save for a few feathers in her armpits and a narrow strip of golden-coloured hair between her legs. Pirta didn't block up the drain when she shaved, unlike me now as I stood in the bathtub. Her legs were soft and smooth even before shaving.

The bathroom tiles steamed up. Pirta was sweating. A couple of times the blade cut through the skin and red pearls dropped into the sea of hair as the tide rose menacingly.

'Hurry up, girls! Your Daddy's got to have his shower,' Mum shouted, banging on the bathroom door.

'My meeting's about to start!'

I gingerly stepped out of the bath. Pirta dabbed my stinging legs with a towel. I stuck my hand into the black sea and scooped hairs out of the plughole. With a gurgle the water drained away, water mixed with blood, but the hairs remained. They wriggled in the vortex like happy little snakes.

Dad opened the door with a set of pincers.

'For the love of Jesus!' he exclaimed.

Mum stood behind him, half-asleep.

'Shall I ring for Tauno?' she asked cautiously.

'I don't want him or any of those other gossipmongers here. I'll clear this shameful mess up myself.'

I withdrew into the sauna as Dad fetched a plastic bag and began stuffing it full of hairs. I sat on the bench and stroked my legs. They were every bit as smooth and beautiful as those of the girl I searched in vain for in the mirror. A gentle touch opened up my pores and the bristly hairs began to push their way out again. They began pushing through in new places too: my chin, my upper lip. The growth there was much thinner and I managed to remove the hairs fairly easily with Mum's tweezers, though plucking stung sharply and made my eyes water. Dad cursed as he took the bag of hairs out to the car. Mum cursed when Dad forced her to take the bag to the dump in the dark.

'Get one of your hussies to take it, why don't you,' she hissed.

By morning the hairs had grown back to form a small pine forest, the tips of which tore holes in my woollen tights. Nature always renewed itself. Soon the tops of the trees would sweep the red-hot winter sky which the cold had frozen into motionlessness.

'This has got to stop!'

A voice came from beneath the ice, a hollow voice that grew in strength and ripped the first crack in the ice. The house shuddered. It hadn't chosen this spot itself. It hated its place by the riverbank, where its façade was under threat every spring. Nobody was there to help when the river turned nasty and hurled snotty lumps at the windows. It was all Grandpa's fault. Grandpa had chosen this spot, but when it was time to stand up and take responsibility he was nothing but a pile of brittle bones in the cemetery, and we couldn't trace his soul.

Uncle was running up and down the street shouting:

'The ice is melting! The ice is melting!'

'Don't talk daft, man. It doesn't thaw in April,' people replied and continued on their way.

The river became angry and spat at them with a vengeance. New cracks appeared. Water began to surge. Soon afterwards, the siren at the fire station went off and church bells rang out and people started building a fire on the bridge to grill their sausages.

'Has it gone mad?' they shouted as the river splashed icy water at their bonfire.

Workplaces emptied. Everyone gathered on the bridge and around the edges of the labyrinth. Some climbed on to the roofs of their houses to watch through binoculars as winter disintegrated into great, heavy blocks of ice which, once freed from their chains, sluiced forth in a furious torrent.

I stood on the riverbank and shouted commands at the river until the water rose up and knocked me over. It calmed for a moment so that I could escape. Only then did it attack the house, flushing out Mum, Dad and Doughnut.

They ran after me panting, water flowing down their coats.

'Quick, Kristina, hide before folk see!'

Only then did I see for myself. My trousers, which had been as white as snow, had turned a dark shade of red.

Sunday

Sunday dinner had been cleared from the table. I cycled down to the café by the customs office. I bought a three-tiered cake with strawberry jam and strawberry jelly and thick dollops of cream between each of the layers. I tried to eat slowly and really savour it, but the cake slipped down into my stomach almost whole. I ordered another cake, then a third. While I was eating the fourth cake the dough began to make its way back up my windpipe, and when I spat it out I saw a clot of congealed blood on the plate.

'Fancy a ride?' Göran hollered from his black car as I cycled back towards the village.

'Not in your shitty car.'

'Don't go, Kristina. They're perverts, them Swedes!' shouted Kari.

The cakes melted into a soft mass as I peddled behind Kari's scooter and round behind the supermarket. Noxious smoke rubbed the film of grease from my mouth. Another wave of nausea swept over me, dizzying me, and I couldn't resist when Kari grabbed me round the waist and pulled me tight against him.

'Kristina, I want to start . . . with you.'

'I've got my period.'

'Your what?'

'Forget it.'

'Okay,' he said and stubbed his cigarette out on the back of his hand.

I stood under the shower until the water ran cold. I then moved over to the bed and gently positioned my bottom on the floral sheets. Whenever I was about to fall asleep, Kari's hands shook me by the hips and blood sprayed all over the walls.

'You little toe-rag,' Mum muttered after I'd stained the upholstery with blood.

She dug a bottle of pills from her apron pocket and emptied it in one gulp. After that, her anger subsided and her eyes glazed over. She shuffled into the bedroom and closed the door behind her. Through the walls I could hear her voice. It had a number of different pitches. It echoed differently depending on what room we were in. The porous logs in the hallway brought out the lower tones, while the cold tiles in the bathroom accentuated the shrill upper notes. The endless space outdoors blended the upper and lower tones so that they rang out together, without ever sounding in harmony.

Inside me was a silence that filtered words from the storm of sounds. They were heavy words and stopped me escaping.

We had gone to Ruuhijärvi where I ate my fill of Grandma's enormous cinnamon buns.

'Kristina, I think we should have a talk,' said Mum.

'Hm?' I muttered, licking the wonderful sticky sugar from my upper lip.

'Kristina, this is serious.'

'Hm?'

'Kristina, you've put on weight.'

'Hm?'

'Do you hear me? Put on weight! Filled out! It's your build, poor girl. You've inherited from me, and I inherited from Grandma. Your bones are just the way they are, you can't change them, but I can save you from fat, Kristina. I'll teach you some moderation.'

'Hm?'

'You've got to watch what you eat. Say no when you're offered things. Eat little bits, chew properly. Eat food that's low in calories, no fat and no sugar. No more cream straight from the tub for you, young lady. Keep an eye on yourself. Eat out of hunger, not greed. Take your time. Eat with your mouth closed and don't make a noise when you swallow. Don't gobble things down and don't stuff yourself. Don't overeat. Only take the amount you need. Make sure your stomach's always left that little bit empty. That way you'll stop eating when you most feel like eating. No more pudding, except on Sundays and at Christmas. Eat regularly, small portions. Drink lots of water, lots at a time. Fast for a day the minute your tummy starts to wobble and your face won't fit in the mirror.'

I swayed in front of the old mirror that hung above Grandma's bed. My chest felt cramped, my trousers were suddenly rough and tight. The room shrank and the mirror grew larger. The girl inside it was small and dainty.

'Don't trust that mirror, it takes at least two kilos off you,' Mum shouted from the kitchen and continued talking to Grandma.

'She's always been a big lass.'

'She's a chubby one, just like you,' said Grandma.

I stared at the floor and tried to hug myself, but my stomach grew and suddenly my arms weren't long enough to hold in the excess within me. They chatted away. My name wasn't mentioned again. The waves carried me inside the mirror and I disappeared. There I was, large and crippled.

Pirta

Pirta lived across the road in a house which, in Grandpa's father's day, used to serve as the wheat store for the village. Since then it had been done up. Extra gables and an upstairs had been built and it had been sold to Pirta's parents. I was born first. Seven months went by, then Pirta was born. Seven years went by, then Pirta's little brother Pessi was born. Around the time of Pessi's birth I learned that they had removed my mum's womb, so rather than a baby I started nagging for a dog instead.

Pirta's dad worked on the railway and her mum in the plastic factory, and my parents didn't want to invite her round to play.

'They've got no values.'

I knew what a value was. It was a cracked piece of crystal that I had picked up from the living room floor after one of the many storms that erupted between Mum and Dad. I kept my treasure in the toy cupboard where I would hide from the sharp voices that rose out of the silence. I sat in the cupboard staring at the floor where a thin beam of light shone in, frail with dust. It illuminated the cupboard in rainbow colours and softened my sinful fingers as they slowly crept along their carpet of skin and down to the forbidden place.

Shivers ran up my spine, all the way up to the top of my head, then cascaded back down in a great waterfall and disappeared in through the golden gates of my navel. As I breathed in, the tremors moved up again and the cycle continued, though my fingers were now stroking Mum's old kimono which I had been allowed to use for dressing up.

I put on the kimono and an enormous hat and walked out of the house pushing my doll's pram. I strolled along the road and nodded ceremoniously at Pirta as she played in their yard. She came running after me and pulled at my sleeve with her sand-coated hands and didn't want to let go.

Pirta followed me back home and started rummaging through my things. She dropped a little dome in which snowflakes were falling on a church. She grabbed my dolls and twisted them into strange poses, oblivious to the pain I felt on their behalf. I ran into the cupboard and only dared come out again once Pirta had left.

Mum peered out at Pirta's house through the slats in the Venetian blinds.

'It's a shitty life they've got,' she proclaimed.

Mum only opened the blinds when she started cleaning. Then Pirta's mum could see that we were hard at work, and sometimes she even responded to the challenge by starting doing her own cleaning. Pirta's dad hauled their rugs out into the yard; they were all threadbare, and when he began beating them they threw up thick clouds of dust that wafted into our house through the walls.

'It's enough to give me an asthma attack,' said Mum.

When I rolled the blinds back down, they drew the curtains at Pirta's place. Her mum was lying on the kitchen floor, her body convulsing, froth spewing from the corner of her mouth.

'Don't you go telling anyone,' Pirta's dad implored her.

Pirta shut herself in her room and rocked beneath the blankets. We swung with our backs to one another until a hurricane burst the foetal membrane and we were born into each other's arms. We had a lot in common. We both hated our parents. Neither of us wanted to play with dolls any more.

'I know.'

'I know too.'

'Your mum's got epilepsy.'

'And your dad sleeps around.'

We stood in the middle of the road and stared at one another in rapture. The curtains twitched in both our windows, but no one spoke of values any longer. Mum just sighed and laid a cold flannel over her eyes. Dad went down to the boiler room, opened the stove door and, as he stoked the fire, flicked open his beer bottle with a hiss.

Trousers

The air conditioning hummed. We were just descending into afternoon tedium when a taxi pulled up outside and jauntily tooted its horn. Dad raced down the stairs and into the hallway. Mum stood in the door, blocking the way as he tried to stagger outside.

'You're not going in those old trousers.'

'Give us a break, woman,' Dad growled.

He looked up at the ceiling as Mum yanked his trousers down to his ankles and told me to fetch a pair of pressed dress trousers from the wardrobe. I picked the ugliest ones I could find. Dad huffed and puffed as Mum forced him into them.

'It's not a fancy do,' he protested.

Mum silenced him with a slap. Outside the taxi tooted a touch more irritably. Dad groaned and Mum laughed. Punishing Dad was the best remedy for her migraines. She beamed with health every time she got to decide what Dad would look like when he went to see his bit on the side.

'You can think what you like,' he muttered, wriggling out from between her legs.

'I don't think anything. Will you do your flies up, man?' she cackled as the taxi driver revved the engine angrily.

The following week Dad turned up for Sunday dinner in a coarse, smart jacket that Mum had bought him. Her eyes twisted into a glassy stare as Dad knelt before her and asked her to turn up his cuffs, which stuck out from beneath his jacket sleeves. It was his way of saying sorry. And Mum forgave him. She rolled up his sleeves and dusted the specks of dandruff from his shoulders. She wet a dishcloth and scoured Dad's face and neck until you could no longer make out his love bites from all the abrasions.

'And there've never been any others?'

'No . . .'

'And nobody in the village clapped eyes on you?'

'No . . .'

'And there's not going to be a next time?'

'No . . .'

'You're sure about that?'

'No . . .'

Mum stood up from the table with a shriek. One large love bite was still uncovered. Mum fetched a wide tie and throttled it around Dad's neck. The tie was covered in pictures of little flies; Mum had chosen it. When all the marks were covered, they kissed. I looked away.

Across the street Pirta looked away as her mum fell back on the sofa, followed quickly by her dad. But there was no disgust in Pirta's eyes. She enjoyed hearing her parents petting and giggling. She didn't know that, before the dark months of winter arrived, her dad would hop on the freight train and run off with another woman, all the way to Oulu. Only much later did disgust set in. And after that she would never dare look down at me again.

Forgiveness was short-lived. The length of time between Dad's dalliances became shorter too. Sometimes there would be marks on his neck after a normal day at work. Mum washed and pressed, washed and pressed, and eventually Dad would stagger back from the neighbour's garage, a bruise on his neck, and claim that there had been nobody there except Tauno, the master home-brewer.

'Change those trousers this minute or I'll string myself up,' Mum screamed.

'Yes, yes,' he assured her.

Mum settled for that. She had slipped into a dark tunnel, at the end of which her migraine blazed. She couldn't see that the man standing in front of her was stark naked.

Stables

'You haven't got a horse any more,' Ina informed me as I stepped into the stable. She was sitting on the edge of Pimu's stall holding a cigarette in the horse's mouth.

'So fucking what?'

Smoked billowed from Pimu's large, moist nostrils.

'Are you fucking mental?' I snapped as I opened the door into Ottilia's stall.

'I wouldn't bother going in there. Pia looks after her now. Pimu's my horse and I'll decide whether or not to give her a smoke.'

Ottilia nudged me with her muzzle and continued eating. I moved a bail of hay to one side and threw the saddle across her back. She shuddered as I tightened the saddle straps, and angrily scraped her hoof across the ground as I forced the frozen bit into her mouth. But she never dared bite me. She respected my firm hands, though I hadn't visited her for months. Pia came cycling into the stable yard just as I pressed my boot into the stirrups and hoisted myself up on to Ottilia's back.

'What the . . . ?'

'You can empty out the shit while I take her for a ride,' I suggested, digging my heels sharply into Ottilia's sides.

From the open stable I could hear the sounds of Ina's cough and Pimu's rasping whinny. Her curses soon dissolved in the wind. The chill bit my ears and thrust its icy fingers through my thin clothes. We trotted along the main road towards the darkening forest. Ottilia didn't bother trying to throw me from her back and calmly obeyed my body's commands. She could sense them long before I was aware of what I wanted, started galloping as soon as we turned on to the dirt track, elegantly jumping over the trees blown over in the storm. The tension in my face and shoulders disappeared. Through the saddle flowed flaming, red smoke that wove its way in through my hips and moved upwards along my spine, making me gabble with contentment.

Ottilia flicked her ears round to listen. She answered with a tired snort. We were the same age, and yet I was young and she was already elderly. I pressed my calves firmly against her sides and pulled on the reins until we came to a standstill and the tears stopped flowing down my cheeks. I loosened the reins and allowed the horse to nibble at the frosted earth. It was early spring and the ground already gave off the scent of new grass. Dandelion roots had come to life. Soon the sun would rise from beneath the soil. I leaned backwards until I could feel the horse's warmth against the back of my head. I crossed my legs around the saddle and let my eyes slowly shut.

The forest drew breath and curled into a foetal position. As it exhaled, the hurricane fled into the distance. Dreams were a mirror in which I was small and serious.

I remembered standing in a strange stable yard,

waving at Dad, who was just turning off the dirt track and on to the main road. I had a bag on my back embroidered with pictures of horses. A long, plastic whip jutted out from one side of the bag. Soon I would be using it to whip my horse, which didn't obey my calves. The riding instructor tutted and swore crudely.

As dusk fell I whimpered with remorse and tried to bite the wicked whip in half. The stall door swung open with a creak and I had to go in with fresh hay and a bucket of water. Horses have a good memory. I knew she would never forget the suffering that my instructor had told me to inflict on her. I didn't shout as the horse turned and started ominously backing up towards me. I kept my lips firmly pursed together as she cornered me against the wall and roughly shuffled her behind at me. I didn't complain when, out in the pasture, she stood on my foot with all her weight, or when, as I was leading her back to the stable, she reared her head and I flew into the air, making the reins cut into my wrists.

The tears only came once we were in the sauna. I was sitting on a low stool, trying not to look at the other girls as they shot me spiteful, malicious glares from the upper benches.

'Can't you talk?' they sneered.

'Yes.'

'Say *aye* or I'll smack your face.'

'*Aye*,' I peeped.

They eventually lost interest and focused on each other.

'Have you ever wanked anybody off?'

'Have you ever fucked anybody?'

'Have you ever given anybody a blow job?'

They were older than me. They had girls' faces but the

bodies of women. They were stupid. I was wise. They sniggered and cackled. They were sinking into a swamp in which I would never set foot. I walked out of the sauna with my body upright, my head held high and proud. I didn't flinch when a ladleful of hot water splashed across my back. I had seen their curly hairs, their pointy tits; I had seen beyond their stupidity. I had seen the safe land which they had lost, but on which I still stood firmly.

This knowledge protected me for the remainder of our camp. The horses made way when I stepped into the stall, stopped playing up at the edge of the field and obediently broke into a gentle gallop. I hid the whip in a pile of hay, and I wasn't even annoyed at Dad when he arrived to pick me up half a day late and tried to flirt with the husky-voiced riding instructor.

Ottilia had stopped eating now. Somewhat stiff with the cold, I forced my body back into a sitting position. Ottilia snorted angrily and broke into a gallop along the main road. I lent forward and held on tightly to her mane until, just before we reached the stable yard, she reared up and threw me from her back.

My thundering head echoed with the sound of Ina and Pia's wicked voices, as I limped home along the main road. Kari was waiting on his scooter at the railway junction.

'Get on,' he commanded.

I climbed on and sat behind Kari. I placed my arms around his waist and held on tight because my head was throbbing and my legs felt powerless.

'I reckon you fancy me,' Kari shouted above the wind.

We drove across the tracks. The train was coming, but Kari didn't want to hang about. He tried to race the train, to escape it, and at the church he turned on to the road to

Lankojärvi. Speed was a haven taking us further away from death. The train began to slow, Kari put his foot down. I begged my fingers not to squeeze him too hard, but they didn't obey me. They pressed themselves through his woollen lumber jacket and into his hips and again he shouted through the wind, but I could no longer make out the words, and he didn't stop, though the road was slippery and he was going far too fast and the tyres skidded over the flat ground. We didn't need words, for a red mist flowed through my fingers, from Kari into me. I could have sat there forever, as long as Kari wanted me to, as long as he let me hold him tightly and accept what flowed within him.

It was better that he didn't speak. His skin was wise; its silence hid the right words. His mouth was not so wise. In his mouth lived a tongue numbed with cigarettes and chewing tobacco, a tongue that reached too far down my throat and formed ugly words.

Once we had turned on to an even smaller road by the bar at Matinlompolo, Kari stopped the scooter and turned to me.

'Fucking hell, Kristina, you've got fat thighs,' he said and kick-started the engine again.

My fingers let go of their own accord. The mist turned to grey smoke. For the rest of the journey my fingers gripped the cold steel panel behind my back. But as we pulled up outside the cottage Kari was already beaming with smiles and happily pinching my thighs. My legs quickly calmed down and carried me into the cottage where the fire had long since gone out and the coals lay cold in the hearth. I didn't recognise the cottage. Kari did, but he couldn't find any wood for the fire; he didn't even really look. He found a bed with a cold embrace. My skin was glowing, but Kari wasn't allowed to know that. I put up a bit of a struggle as he tore at my clothes; I refused to take off my puffer jacket. The button on my trousers was too tight for him. He started pinching me through my clothes. The bed quickly warmed up. Kari's tongue forgot to say anything; it didn't have a chance. It searched and searched until my tongue gave in, came out of its hiding place, licked Kari's tongue until the taste of tar had been dispelled, turned into something different, something new. Our tongues played and our hands struggled with one another. Kari's hands won, made my hand touch his jeans, his flies, taut across a hard bulge. One little touch and the bulge exploded. Through the fabric seeped something moist and cloying. The bulge was suddenly soft again. Now my finger dared to touch it, dared to feel around, dared go inside and explore that already familiar woodland, but the bed was too hot. Sweat poured beneath my puffer jacket and Kari's tongue fled and didn't show itself again. The door slammed. Black wisps rose behind the window. They came flooding out of Kari's mouth and from the top of his head and his tongue began forming words again.

'Fucking hell, Kristina, look what you've done to me.'

'What have I done?' I asked.

Thick smoke rose from the chimney. I quickly shut the flue and ran outside before the smoke could kill me. Kari kick-started the scooter. Back on the road a car drove towards us, slowed down, and pairs of eyes stared out at us.

'Cover your face,' Kari hollered above the wind. 'I don't know whose cottage it was.'

My fingers gripped the orange wool once again. Happy fingers. The fat around my thighs tightened with joy, almost melted away. There was no reason to be afraid of a boy who was so scared that he'd wet himself. The smell still hung in the air, the wind couldn't blow it away. The warm, gentle wind, an envoy of summer.

Sperm

'We snogged.'

'And?'

'Touched.'

'Underneath?'

'No, through his clothes.'

'Fucking tight-arse.'

'You should know.'

'So did anything happen?'

'A bit.'

'What?'

'He pissed himself.'

'Pissed?'

'In his pants.'

'You've got to be kidding?'

'That's what I thought.'

'What's wrong with you?'

'With *him*?'

'With *you*. You don't get anything, do you? It wasn't piss.'

'What?'

'It was *sperm*.'

'How d'you know?'

'It's what boys do. Aslak does it too.'

I ran across the street and back home. I placed the ladder next to the bookcase and started reading. The top shelves contained books my parents didn't want me to read. I had secretly read them all, but there were some things I hadn't quite understood. I spent all day standing on the ladder reading. I read until I knew. By evening Mum shook me down from my tower.

'Don't say it's quantum physics again? You'll lose your wits like that.'

'Let the lassie read. She's got more sense in her head that you,' said Dad, taking my side.

'I wouldn't talk about sense with your brain.'

'And I wouldn't open my trap if my breath smelt of chemicals.'

'Why don't we open the window and let the neighbours hear too?'

'I'll open it if you promise to jump out, okay?'

'You jump yourself, straight down the pub.'

'Thanks for reminding me.'

I hid the medical book behind some other books, and carrying my physics books I marched into my room. I spread the book out on my bed and called Pirta.

'Do you know what's left of you?'

'If what?'

'If you fall.'

'Where?'

'Into a black hole.'

'Not this again.'

'Light.'

'Nothing else?'

'Nothing else.'

'All right. You win.'

'You won't blab to anyone?'

'No.'

Pirta's voice was tired. Behind her voice there was nothing. I pulled the curtains apart, just to make sure that Aslak's bike wasn't propped up outside Pirta's house. Dad was peddling into the village at a rate of knots. Standing in the doorway, Mum shouted after him.

'You forgot to brush your teeth!'

I quickly turned the lock in my door, as soon as the front door banged and Mum's sobs began moving up the stairs. This night was mine, this night brightening with the pull of summer. It didn't matter that the house was full of anger. Through my body flowed love, blood-red and cleansing.

Abyss

Kari followed his own path. If I couldn't find him under the bridge to Sweden, where the village winos had set up camp, I knew to make my way towards the railway tracks. He sat there with a watch and a notepad, his eyes glazed, staring at the horizon. When the ground began to shudder, he took a deep breath and felt the train come crashing through him. Only after it had gone past did his eyes focus, and I plucked up the courage to approach him.

'Give us a smoke,' he commanded.

I dutifully handed him the box of cigars I'd stolen from Dad. Kari's crooked smile made my stomach acid fizz. He lit a cigar and mouthed thick smoke signals up into the sky; Pirta and Aslak soon appeared from the woods, and I no longer had to worry that Kari might pull me tight against him and harden beneath his flies and say:

'Fucking hell, Kristina, I want something more.'

I wasn't exactly sure what it was he wanted. It must have had something to do with the black little adders that wriggled beneath my belly button, squeezed inside my jeans, which were already too tight. Perhaps he wanted to set them free. Aslak knew that, one night, a woman had crawled into Kari's bed, a woman who wasn't his mother but who, given her age, might as well have been. She had instructed Kari to climb on top of her and dive down into the abyss, black and moist, and as Kari floundered up and down along its walls the woman had started to snore, and her breath was so heavy with the scent of liquor that Kari too had become intoxicated and hadn't wanted to be sober since.

Kari wanted to dive back into the abyss.

Any abyss, for that matter. Even mine, dark and cramped, regardless of the thorn-bushes growing along its sides – something only Doughnut and I knew anything about.

I doubt Doughnut still remembered. He was only a puppy back then, and the thorns nothing but soft lint. He had caught the scent of the dark place hidden within me, though as yet I had no knowledge of it myself. I didn't have time to stop him as he leapt across the ground and licked my genitals with his little tongue until the gates opened and, as if of their own volition, my fingers swam into the magnificent kingdom below.

There I lay at the end of my fingers; me, whole, complete and happy inside myself, while Doughnut whined dejectedly behind the door. He had no business in my bed after that, once the underwater paradise had become a reality there in my bedroom. At least not while I was playing with myself, breathing in the room's dust, hoping for the moment of death to linger, to last until the floor began to shake and the sun thrust its cold beams through the slats of the blinds.

Waking up was always frightening. As I walked towards the bathroom my pores would gauge the atmosphere in the house. Every hair stood on end whenever going into the kitchen wasn't a good idea. Mum stood by the cooker, her eyes puffy from weeping, stirring porridge with not enough water in it. She stirred and stirred until the porridge resembled a thick adhesive that not even Doughnut could stomach.

Offended, he trotted along behind me and whimpered behind the door as I opened my legs and, trembling with pleasure, expelled the last remnants of death from the walls of the abyss.

'What *are* you up to in there?' Dad asked from behind the door.

When I opened the door Mum gave me a stern look and filled Doughnut's bowl with rancid milk.

'Iris rang. Says you've been bullying Pessi.'

'I wasn't. It was Pirta.'

The lie slipped out of my mouth quickly, spun like a fireball from one corner of the room to the other and cleansed the air. Mum stretched and came back to life. Dad puckered his lips and whistled merrily. Doughnut threw up in his bowl, then ate the vomit. There was no greater sin than telling a falsehood. I had been told this hundreds of times. It was my duty to tell my parents everything. It was my duty to keep all the secrets with which I had been entrusted. It was my duty to remain within the boundaries of the truth.

If ever I deviated from the truth, there would be Punishment. A crushing weight rested on the very word.

I preserved the truth inside me, then spat it in the face

of the first passer-by. I talked to teachers, friends, friends' parents, the reindeer, the trees, the winos under the bridge to Sweden. I talked about everything I had heard.

'You've an overactive imagination,' the teachers claimed.

'You've a cheek, shaming your parents like that.'

'But Mum doesn't want to have sex any more and Dad just can't take it!' I shouted, the urge to cry choking me.

And so again I ended up in the bully circle.

'Liar! Liar!' they chanted and pulled my trousers down round my ankles.

That made me shut my mouth. I didn't belong inside the bully circle. I belonged with the leaders, whose job it was to drag the weaklings to one side and think of an insult to make tears tickle their throats and piss run down their trouser legs.

I was born to be a torturer, not to be humiliated, and I quickly learned how to be calculating. If the truth about my parents was too unbelievable, I turned it on its head and into a liberating lie. As I encountered admiration and curiosity, I allowed stories to grow until I was no longer sure what I had originally been told. Was Mum hurt that Dad had been flirting with one of her friends, or was Dad angry because Mum had pissed in his barrel of home-brew? Who had lashed out first? Had Dad shoved his head through the painting Mum had inherited or had she stuck him in the gut with a paper knife?

Admiration turned all too easily to suspicion. If the circle began to form around me, I would sneak out of school in the middle of the afternoon and join Pessi playing in the yard. I ran after him as he shot his play gun at imaginary enemies, and told him all the stories that were bursting out of me.

'Amazing,' Pessi rejoiced as the enemy fell down dead.

I lifted him on to my shoulders and gave him a piggy-back until words ran out. He slipped down my back and pestered me to let him down. I took him round the back of the house and set him down to roll about amongst the pine cones. At first he laughed. Then he cried. I only stopped when he swore he believed everything I'd said was true.

Freight train

My jodhpurs were too tight around the thighs and backside. The legs were too short. The suede patches that I had been so proud of were now worn and tattered. But Mum, who had positioned herself between me and the mirror, was beaming and full of energy.

'Riding about's no good for a young lady.'

She turned to face the mirror and adjusted her hair, which she wore in a bun.

'Bouncing up and down on an old nag with your legs akimbo – just look at yourself! You'll twist yourself out of shape yet, girl. Your hips are all shoved forwards. You'll soon be walking with your crotch thrust out like a man or . . .'

'Like what?' Dad asked, placing himself between Mum and the mirror.

'Like one of your harlots, your tarts and your whores!'

Dad fixed his hair, currying it back in shiny clumps.

'Don't you call your daughter a whore,' he said firmly.

'For the love of God, your father's dyed his hair,' Mum shrieked.

‘And I’ll do it again if the fancy takes me.’

I took a deep breath. A button flew off my trousers leaving a small crack in the mirror.

‘I’ve stopped riding,’ I said, pulling a face.

In the mirror’s reflection Mum and Dad stood fragmented, their limbs and features criss-crossing together.

‘And what are you doing now then?’ asked Dad’s mocking voice.

‘You might ask yourself that,’ Mum replied.

I stepped out of my trousers before Mum could tell me to, and disappeared into my room to try on another pair. They were tight too, but the fabric began to give after I did a few dance steps. The throaty voice of Pelle Miljoona helped my body to relax and stretch.

Sister, just this one night with you, I sang along with him.

The door flew open. Mum stood in the doorway, her hair fallen from its bun.

‘Do you hear what they’re saying?’ she shouted, pulling her hair out.

‘They spend the night together.’

‘They spend the night in bed together, then he never comes home at night again – never.’

‘I will, I promise I will,’ Dad shouted.

The door slammed shut and the familiar, damp silence fell once again.

Silence allowed Mum the space to sob, but it hid within me, letting out vicious, whistling sounds; I couldn’t make them stop, though once Mum had left I dared turn the music back up. This time Pelle consoled me more cautiously, more quietly. There was no reason to anger a house that hoarded silence in its very building material. Sometimes the silence was light, as light as my being before I was conceived and attached to the house, which became heavier with each new flood, more and more saturated with salty sadness.

When silence descends, heavy and wet, nobody has the right to turn it away.

The tracks ran close to the house and shortly before midnight, just as the freight train was approaching the village, my dreams turned restless. They flew from the bed and darted around the room and didn't look out for my head as they hit against the thick stone walls. I only curled up beneath the sheets once sleep had released its grip and my eyes opened. Every night I fought against the tremors. Every night. I gritted my teeth together and focussed all my energy so that it might not happen, that it might not crush me, that just once it might pass me by.

The train came crashing through my head, juddering and clattering, and only pulled into the station once I was already in pieces. The railway workers' shouts lacerated my eardrums. My chest trembled as hefty logs rolled from the trailer on to the ground. Only once the train continued on its journey did the trembling stop and I could drift back to sleep. In the morning I tried to convince myself that nothing had happened.

Nothing had happened before either, when I'd floated, almost weightless, in front of the big mirror in the hallway upon hearing the train's first piercing night cries. When Black Pete arrived on the train and stepped through the mirror into the house, he wrapped me in thick rope that glowed in the dark, that never ended. He wrapped me in rope until I was invisible beneath it.

During the daytime I would cycle along the tracks, and a quick glance at the forecourt was enough to prove that I had indeed already been there. I knew exactly how much wood had come off the trailers and which of the railway workers had been on night shift. If Tauno had been working the previous night, he was nowhere to be seen in the morning, so I dared smoke the cigarette Kari had taken from his mother's pocket after she had passed out.

Kari puffed out a great big smoke ring and jumped through it on to the tracks. Pirta snatched up a jotter, in which Kari had noted the arrival and departure times of all the trains, and started shouting:

'Get off the tracks! The train's coming! Off the tracks!'

I dived on to the tracks and wrenched Kari on to the verge. His heart hammered frenziedly against my chest as the train shot past.

'You love me,' he panted and burst into tears.

The train had gone.

Pirta's jumper came up to her ears. She and Aslak disappeared behind the pile of logs. I opened my mouth and Kari disappeared inside me. He flowed within me as I walked home with my hair, stinking of tobacco and gravel, blown across my face. My lips still felt the touch of Kari's teeth.

The house's breath was hot and fragrant. For the first time in ages, Mum had heated up the oven and baked enormous buns, their centres filled with melted butter and sugar. I had a habit of sticking my tongue deep into the buns and sucking out their sweet filling. Mum had a habit of giving me disapproving looks. But now her happy cheeks glowed and her eyes invited me to gobble up as many buns as I wanted. When I declined, her shoulders drooped and disappointment spread in heavy lines across her face. She picked up one of the buns, the most misshapen in the row, and crumbled it into her cup. Her coffee was steaming and grey, and she slurped it loudly as if this would prevent her from burning her tongue. Dad came into the kitchen, snatched up a pile of buns and crammed them into his mouth.

'Don't smack your chops,' Mum snapped.

Dad closed his mouth, chewed a few times, then swallowed. His throat gave out a low gurgle that brought Kari's soft voice to my ear:

'Come and die with me!'

'No.'

'If you don't, somebody else will.'

He was lying on the tracks, flat on his back, imagining that the train would pass over him and he could lie in his own little space and survive unscathed. It was possible. A boy in a film had done it. After careful measurements he had lain down on the tracks, let the train run over him, then sat up wiping the soot from his face.

'Come and die with me!'

It was my voice in Kari's mouth. Too weak. Too long a journey to the new birth that people called death. Too few people died around me, and those who did were taken quickly, shut in a cold cellar, in a dark coffin, buried before anyone had time to grieve properly, let alone rejoice at the possibility of meeting again, in a new form, in new conditions, in a new kind of light.

As Mum lay in bed, Dad suddenly started busying himself. He poured himself drinks. He cleared up and did the laundry and washed himself after spending the night with one of his women. He went through my homework and played Monopoly with me. Sometimes he would ask me to pour him a drink. I poured cranberry juice and crushed ice into a glass and mixed in a healthy lug of vodka so that he would become sleepy and motionless; so he'd be like Mum.

They both slipped away and I had the place to myself. Their wishes faded, giving me back my freedom. I could wander around the house and switch on all the lights. I could smoke in the boiler room and blow the smoke right into Dad's heart as it blazed in the fireplace. They didn't want to see my bitter smoke. I admired them and wanted to be like them; I despised them because they didn't realise that I was their equal. I was hung over on Sunday mornings, just like Dad. After mixing Dad's cranberry drink, I poured into my glass of fizzy orange a measure of vodka strong enough to mess with my brain.

Once Dad had fallen asleep, I sat staring at the television. We watched *Happy Days* on a Saturday night. I scratched Dad's leg, which lay asleep in my lap, and disappeared inside the television's electric field and into Fonzie's musky embrace. In the morning I sprawled in bed until the revulsion had shrunk into oblivion, along with the excesses of Saturday night. A string of hymns, the sacred product of so many bleeding vocal cords, flowed from the radio into every room in the house; Mum drew strength from this as she cleaned up, her eyes framed in red blotches. Sighing heavily, Dad staggered behind the string from one room to the next. I didn't dare breathe, for behind the front door stood a black phantom, the spawn of death before its final exile. The phantom frightened naughty children and adults who hadn't made their way to the village church for Sunday communion. Those who scare others are the most afraid of all.

Nan

In the summer Dad and I trundled over to visit Nan in Inari. After Grandad died, Nan had gone soft. Grandad's spirit flowed warm inside her; I didn't want to resist as it sucked me inwards. I sat in the car next to Dad and my trust in him made his eyes glisten with happiness, and throughout the whole, long journey, he didn't once stop to pop into the off-licence.

Nan was waiting on the steps. It seemed as though she had been waiting there all day, all year, all her life, ever since Grandad had passed on. She lived in a small cottage which, in my imagination, had grown into a golden palace complete with marble staircases and Nan sitting at the top in a ball-gown laced with diamonds.

Nan opened her arms and didn't allow us into the house until we had allowed her to give us a kiss. I stepped into the kitchen as though it were a great temple. Nature seemed to approach me through windows the size of the wall and reach out its hand by way of a greeting. At Nan's place I could slouch by the fire prodding burning embers with a poker, and nobody would force me to go outside, even though the sun was shining and the forest was bursting with berries waiting to be eaten.

Nobody forced me, and that's why I went. Nan didn't ask where I was going or when I would be back. She simply reminded me not to disturb the animals. Before stepping into the forest I had to stop at the gate, grow and protect those I didn't know at all. When you grow you become hungry and the forest offers its body in all its abundance. I ate light-green spruce shoots and delicate birch leaves, and as summer burst into flower I gorged on fat cloudberries, whose fiery potency protected me from the winter cold. In the autumn, blueberries swelled to the touch and filled me to the brim.

I wasn't afraid, though I knew that the bears hadn't yet retreated into hibernation – of course I knew that – and that reindeer bulls, maddened with the onset of autumn, might attack me with their giant antlers. I had Nan's blessing and kisses, and even with my eyes closed I could climb up the hillside and find a path, hidden beneath the heather, leading to a mountain spring.

I lay on my stomach, breathing carefully so as not to shatter the mirror-like surface of the water. The decayed leaves of bygone years gleamed back through my reflection from the bottom of the pool. The spring thought I was beautiful, and I wanted never to let go of that moment. I didn't want to see the spiral twisting towards the surface; I didn't want to see my face as my own hand pierced through the surface and scooped water up to wet my lips. I didn't want to see the boy who rose from the spring and stared at me with grimacing, squinty eyes.

'Fucking hell, Kristina, you're crazy,' said the boy.

I hurled a handful of black peat at his face and he disappeared. The pool turned brown as the wind stirred the water with its paws. The bluethroats chirped in distress as I ran through their nesting ground and past the old reindeer fences, down the hillside and back towards Nan's cottage where comforting smoke billowed from the chimney.

Nan was sitting on the steps wringing her hands.

'Don't go in there,' she said firmly.

But I was already inside, in the darkened cottage, where, on reindeer skins laid out on the floor, Dad was kissing a woman.

Throughout the journey home I could see Dad's furrowed brow in the rear-view mirror, and Nan's tear-stained face on the inside of my eyelids. Dad took a bottle out of the glove compartment and emptied it in a single swig. The next time I opened my eyes the world was upside down. I was dangling uncomfortably from my seatbelt, staring at Dad's ruddy neck.

'Don't tell a soul,' he sobbed.

Skin

Blood didn't scare me any more. It was a familiar sight. It trickled from scratches and wounds, and built up behind thick scabs. All over Kari's body blood formed fascinating, forbidden patterns and I followed them with my fingers and my tongue, until Kari pushed me away from him with both hands.

'Stop it. It tickles.'

When he laughed he was beautiful, almost girl-like. I was so taken aback that I started drawing the knife back and forth across my stomach. Some of the blood-rivers became too deep; they began to flood and stained my clothes.

'Sissy,' I heard Pirta's mocking voice say, but as my face twisted in pain Kari turned serious again.

I laughed with relief as he took off his shirt and rolled it into a ball to stem one of the flooding furrows. He was himself again, the same handsome, fox-eyed Kari with whom I had fallen in love. Not the weak Kari, the sissy that Pirta could sweep out of her life at any moment. Kari could laugh, but not too much, not so that his eyes squinted and his hair went frizzy. At least not while Pirta was watching, because Pirta was spiteful and thought Aslak was better than Kari, more of a man, she said, even though Aslak had a whiny voice and pink stripes in his hair.

My skin liked Kari's laugh. If Pirta was far away, and wasn't about to turn up, my skin dared to open up and suck in the warmth flowing from Kari's soft, playful fingers. When his laughter died away, his fingers became hard and my skin retreated into a small cupboard where the air quickly turned sour. At times like that you had to straighten your clothes quickly, run into the nearest forest and rub your skin against a tree trunk until the dirt of shame was gone and the skin could breathe once more.

Kari ran after me and took out his knife. The woods behind the flats were restless. Men who had lost their homes slept there. Old Veijo Raappana would flash his genitals at me from behind a big spruce tree if I went there alone. Kari protected me from any bad men. He wanted to protect me.

'Just say the word, and I'll kill your old man.'

I kissed him quickly so that he wouldn't see the horror on my face. It would be good if my parents died. The house would be mine, but what would happen to Kari? He would be taken away from the village and driven down to the open prison in Ylitornio. No. Kari mustn't stain his knife with Dad's blood. It was better that he used his knife to shred up old photographs. Photographs of me on Dad's lap, or of me popping fishes' air bladders with a knife. Or photos of me in a swimming costume washing rugs on the shores of the lake at Ruuhijärvi. Photos of other boys he could leave in peace. Kari knew that, before him, I had dated Ilkka and Aki. Kari wasn't the jealous type. He only hated the photographs in which my life looked better than his. Everything I had been given that he didn't have was something lost from our relationship; my job was to make up for the wrongs he had suffered. I let him climb in through the window once Mum and Dad were safely on the other side of my locked door, and handed him the photographs. He went through them quickly, hatefully, and tore them to pieces.

He didn't listen when I told him that sitting in Dad's lap wasn't nice, that Dad puckered his lips and kissed me only after he had first kissed his bottle of cognac. My face stank after Dad's kisses and it took a long time for the smell to evaporate.

'Not everybody can afford to drink cognac,' he muttered bitterly and stabbed his knife through Dad's face.

He waited under the bed as I crept into Dad's office looking for his wallet.

'I've got to get to Sweden. Now,' Kari yelled.

They didn't run into one another. I watched out of the window as Kari ran down the road without stopping to look back. Kari didn't see Dad, who was creeping out of the front door, his shoes in his hands, and Dad didn't see Kari either. Dad glanced up at Mum's window, and from the look of victory in his eyes I could tell that this time her curtains hadn't twitched.

I started a bonfire on my bedroom floor with the shredded photographs. I put out the flames with a quilt once the photographs had curled into a pile of ash. I had saved Dad's life, but he didn't have the faintest idea.

That's why I stole money from him.

That's why at the corner of the house the wind sighed with Mum's voice, a black mantra that hardened around our shoulders.

'I'll kill you.' She said it to Doughnut, but she was looking at me.

Before Doughnut the position of family dog had been held by Beefsteak, a good-natured mongrel who lost his marbles when I was born and started crawling after him and yanking at his fur. He scraped my scalp with his sharp teeth, and when I learned to stand up he would knock me down and trample on my little body.

'Retarded mutt!' Dad proclaimed.

Dad took Beefsteak into the woods, threw him a stick and shot him in the back of the head. An act like this soon becomes a curse. All the pets that entered our house after Beefsteak died a premature death. Sometimes I would feed and look after them, but the end was inevitable. Our Japanese house mouse choked to death on the wood shavings I had laid out to soften its little bed. A tame squirrel drowned in its drinking bowl. A rabbit was paralysed after spending a winter's night in its outdoor cage, fifty degrees below freezing.

Behind the house there was a mass grave that swallowed up all my pets. I covered their bodies with earth and sang a few hymns. Then I forgot about them and started waiting. I called animals, and they would come to me. My parents' protests came to nothing. An animal I have called can't be turned away once it's already standing in the doorway.

And there stood Doughnut. I had rescued him from a floating block of ice and carried him back to the house to recover from the cold with which the river had branded his paws. Mum looked at the dog impassively. Dad gave a dull nod of the head.

A thin furrow ran along the edge of our torpor, allowing

Mum's tears to flow in an uninterrupted stream. She sobbed and sniffled. She never stopped crying. Doughnut jumped up on her and licked the tears from her face. She burst into laughter, but once she noticed the filthy paw-prints on the front of her blouse she angrily shoved him away.

'I'll wring that dog's neck,' she snapped.

I yanked on Doughnut's collar and attached the leash. I gave a sharp tug and he was forced to follow me. Once we were in the woods I removed the collar and asked for forgiveness. I told him to go, to run away and escape, to turn into a wild dog, grow sharp teeth and kill everything that came crashing into the forest. Doughnut stared at my hand, expecting me to throw him a stick. I picked up a stone and threw it at him. He darted away, but the stone struck him on the back. He gave a yelp. I fell to my knees and battered the stone against my forehead. Doughnut started to howl when he saw that I was injured. He howled as I ran away from him, blood trickling into my eyes.

'Go, stupid! Run away!' I cried.

At the edge of the woods I stopped and put his collar back on. I pulled my woolly hat down to protect my bloody forehead and walked along the roadside back to the village. Doughnut was pulling on the leash. A moment ago he had wanted to go back to prison. Now he wanted out again. I no longer wanted to let him go.

'Take your mutt and piss off!' Kari shouted.

I ran with Doughnut to the yard outside the flats and tied his leash around the bicycle stand. I gently stroked his head and begged him to stop whining, but when Kari stuck his head out of the window I kicked the dog in the ribs.

This appeased Kari. He told me to come back inside. I was allowed to sit on the edge of his bed with my hand on his thigh as he tuned his guitar. Even Kauko Röyhkä's voice paled in comparison to Kari's. Kari's voice was even gruffer and caressed the skin beneath my clothes even more softly than Kauko's hand. Sometimes Kari's voice was nothing but a gruff whisper. I was the only one to hear it. It came out of him when words didn't want to come, when he felt too down, when even I was too much for him, and I had to shut myself in the cupboard so that he wouldn't get angry.

He got angry almost every time he laid eyes on Doughnut. I came up with a variety of ways to placate him. I didn't want to leave Doughnut at home. Whenever he was with me, Mum and Dad had no reason to suspect that I was at the flats. I was down at the running track, and I'd get lots of pocket money, which I used to buy tender words and kisses from Kari. Kari loved me. His eyes and hands told me this, though his lips couldn't always say it. Kari loved me, and he didn't really hate Doughnut. He hated his mother, who had never allowed him to keep pets.

As a little boy Kari had always wanted a reptile. He borrowed books on lizards from the library and built a large terrarium all by himself. Nonetheless, the terrarium remained empty. Raakel flushed down the toilet all the lizards Kari had captured in the garden, then one day the terrarium was gone too. Raakel had a new jumper and a guilty look in her eyes, but Kari didn't say a word. A lizard's tongue lived in his mouth, and on it grew a sac of venom. One word to Raakel would have ruptured the sac. Raakel would have died and Kari would have wound up in a cell with his father.

There was something else in the sac too. When Doughnut jumped up on Kari and started licking his face, a small hole appeared in the sac. Drops of venom seeped out, making Kari froth with curses. I accepted these curses like a refreshing shower of rain. They brought with them Kari's spirit, which kept me alive when my own lungs refused to work. What did it matter if the air was black and smelly? And so Kari was tender and gentle, and instead of his guitar he took me in his arms and plucked tones from my skin, tones I had known before my birth into darkness but which had long been forgotten. From this music grew a face that no one had seen before, my own face from the time when I was still floating in oblivion and hadn't yet selected a body in which to make my home.

'Fucking hell, Kristina, you're a bonny lass,' Kari whispered and I forgave him, for everything.

I forgave him for the fact that, of all my relatives, the only one he accepted was Uncle. When Grandpa was still alive, Uncle spent a long time locked in a dark room, and at night he was tied to the end of the bed with a rope. He didn't struggle. He and his calculations were happy almost anywhere. If his imprisonment lasted long enough, another voice appeared alongside the counting. This voice commanded and compelled him, forced him to move. When Grandpa died the ropes were taken off and Uncle walked out of the house. He walked around the lake. He walked along the road to the village. He walked from the village to the next village. Sometimes he would stop at people's houses and ask for something to drink. And he talked endlessly, though Grandma had told him not to.

Nobody refused Uncle their help. It was clear that, once he had had a drink, he would be on his way again, no matter what the weather. He walked through the freezing cold. He walked through baking heat. He walked through torrential rain. He walked against the icy wind. He walked. People laughed at him. He marked his territory with his feet, conquered the village just as single-mindedly as Kari measured the railway tracks.

They were both spurred by the same impulse.

Fainting

I kept my underpants on whenever I had to go in the sauna with Mum. I threw lots of water on the stove so she wouldn't see how mountainous I was becoming. Silently I listened to her thoughts, which all had something to do with men. It didn't matter to whom she compared him, Dad always came out second best. Mum agreed with the hospital caretaker, the headmaster and Tauno.

There was no apparent order of merit in her thoughts. All men were equal, except Dad.

'It's a twisted life,' she muttered, but she could never straighten me out.

Mum wanted me to grow long hair, as long as hers, and I sat there obediently as she tied my hair in a tight bun on the top of my head. She wouldn't allow me to be like Pirta, who looked like a boy with her close-cropped hair. Mum thought Pirta was ugly. She would have thought so even if her hair had been long and flowing, her freckles golden and her eyes glowing like balls of marble concealing a bright blue flame.

Pirta was most beautiful when she was crying.

'Dad's disappeared,' she whispered.

Aslak shoved Pirta to the ground and licked the tears from her face.

'Good job too, he won't be lurking around here any more,' he consoled her.

I stared at the ground. So did Kari.

'An extra train,' he muttered.

Kari had relented. I dared raise my eyes.

Aslak stuck his tongue in Pirta's mouth. I followed Kari up the embankment and along the tracks back to the village.

'The train's not coming, is it?'

'Not yet.'

'When, then?'

'Not yet.'

Kari ran off towards the railway bridge, which crossed the river about a kilometre before the station. I ran after him, though I could already feel the ground trembling.

'Stop! Are you crazy?'

The wind made Pirta's voice sound thin. I bounded over the bridge behind Kari, and jumped on to the embankment on the other side at the very moment the train shot out of the forest. Sucked in his wake, I rolled down the side of the stony verge.

'I made it, I fucking made it!' he panted into my ear.

The train roared past. Its heat relaxed me, melted me. Kari dropped his jotter, crawled on top of me and stuck his tongue in my mouth; it tasted of tobacco. Laughter disappeared down my throat to the bottom of my stomach, and from my vagina deep into the earth. My clothes were damp. The train was already far away, but my body still felt its tremors. Pirta's fingers were shaking as she lit a cigarette and stuck it in my mouth; Kari had already retreated and returned to his jotter. The filter was squashed and moist, the smoke hot and dry. As the train pulled out of the station the earth shook once more and my stomach churned. Vomit flew from Pirta's mouth.

'Dad, Dad,' she sobbed.

The cigarettes ran out. We moved into the bike-shed next to the flats. Pirta was upset, so we let her go first. She sat on her haunches next to the wall.

We played a game called Fainting. It had first become popular in Tornio and had quickly spread to the villages in the north. Kids played this game when they didn't have enough money for drink. First you had to sit on your haunches and start panting. Panting was free, and it was useful. It banished all other thoughts and cleared your head. You had to sit on your haunches and pant until everything started to blur, then you stood up suddenly while the others pressed your chest until you fainted. If you played Fainting too often something in your head might burst. In the hospital in Karunki there was a girl who'd never woken up, though her friends had waited and waited. She was still breathing though.

Pirta panted a hundred times. When she stood up, her face was white.

'Don't die, babe,' Aslak whispered as he pressed his hands firmly against her chest.

Pirta fell backwards and our soft hands protected her, stopping her head from hitting the cement floor. We stood around her in a circle as she dreamt, her eyelids twitching; dreams that took her away from the village, far along the tracks, away from this moment, further than her father had ever dared go; further than the tracks themselves.

Pirta floated away. The sadness was gone. In its place there was light, glowing with magnificent colours which her transformed mind produced in abundance. We paced up and down, imprinting a circle of blood on the cement floor, until Pirta's sleep suddenly snapped and she was born into our arms, her eyes wide with love.

'Amazing,' she gasped and took Kari's place in the circle.

I journeyed first with Kari, then with Aslak, and when it was finally my turn my head opened up and a cloudless sky filled my being. I didn't have to pant for long before the room began to tilt. The bikes started rolling towards me, but I escaped them and fled deep inside the walls as firm pairs of hands crushed my chest.

There were many hands when I awoke on the floor after that long spell of emptiness; curious hands which, without causing pain, examined the corridors of my body.

Migraine

Blows showered down on Doughnut. He was howling outside in his kennel, and nobody but I understood his language, not even the other local dogs whose owners would go out one by one to beat them into silence. While children and wives were beaten behind closed doors, it was acceptable to beat dogs if they disturbed your sleep. So Dad would get himself wound up, whip the belt from his trousers and stride across the yard to Doughnut's kennel.

Dad regularly felt the need to vent his anger. Doughnut howled continually. He wanted to sleep in a warm bed. I missed him as much he missed me, and on the nights when Dad locked him in the kennel we cried for one another. I wailed silently, because my days were busy, full of yearning to be with Kari. But it was Doughnut's cries that reached me. It was as if he knew, he could predict that my happiness wouldn't last long, that a belt buckle would smash it to nothingness once it grew too loud.

I couldn't get to sleep the night after the fainting. I crept into Doughnut's kennel and placed my hands on his ribs as they smarted with pain. He licked my face and bestowed his dreams upon me.

I was a puppy. My mother stood gnawing the ground, her body swaying as her fur fell out in clumps. I had crawled out, and with faltering legs I stood beneath her belly and sucked milk from her sweet nipples. The milk from my dream flowed through my hands into Doughnut as he whimpered in his sleep.

'Your Daddy's a good man. Remember that,' said Mum. She was sitting on the windowsill, her face grey, staring out through the chinks in the blinds. I muttered something in agreement. She cast me a thankful glance, walked into the bedroom and slid beneath the quilt, careful not to crease Dad's untouched side of the bed.

They pulled at me like an elastic rope. My fibres began to fray. Blood rushed to my brain and my veins twisted painfully as they pulled me in different directions. Mum's carer and Dad's confidante. I did my best to make a success of the job that was my birthright.

As a child I fitted comfortably in between them. I would lie silently between them in the double bed, thus preventing Dad from sliding his hand over to Mum's side. Dad's hands were dirty and his breath stank. Mum reminded me of this when I wondered why she always shunned his advances.

Her migraine erupted when Dad returned home after one of his jaunts, which this time had lasted weeks, and took off his smelly boots. He washed his own socks and disinfected his boots, but Mum's head went berserk and had scarcely returned to normal when Dad got itchy feet again. After his hundredth jaunt, Mum's serotonin finally dried up.

'It's the body's own medicine,' she said and spent months in bed. By the end of her sick leave she could no longer take care of her job. She had to make do with temporary jobs, which always seemed to come up just when the silver hammer had started slowly tapping away at her glass forehead and when my hands were numb from all the massaging. On the rare occasions she did go to work, she would take with her a large handbag and stuff it full of pills. If she ran out of pills before her next job, she would send me to the hospital. I knew how to pick the lock on the medicine cupboard as I repeated the line Mum had taught me:

'Mum forgot her cardigan. It's in the staff room.'

I believed Mum. When she lied, it wasn't really lying. When she hit me, it wasn't really hitting. It was a misunderstanding.

Mum was sad when I first started school. I remembered how she wept all the way as we walked through the woods to the school building. While we were eating breakfast, Dad had come back from one of his night-time visits without his trousers, and Mum needed my support.

Mum wept as she left me in the classroom. She wasn't interested in the teacher's careful enquiries, but slumped against the door as soon as he had closed it behind her. Her tears flowed beneath the door, soaking the teacher's socks.

Mum wept when the teacher opened the door and asked her to leave.

She wept when the teacher locked the door and left her outside.

She cried my name as the whole school ran out into the playground to watch her being dragged into an ambulance.

I tried to go with her, but the teacher walked me firmly back into the classroom.

'Kristina's mum's a bit doolally,' he declared.

A woman from the mental health clinic came round to

the house and said that Dad ought to take more responsibility and bang his fists on the table if need be. Mum slowly recovered, but my friends never forgot. They called me names until I dared resort to using my own fists, which, while looking after Mum, had turned into stones.

With time I gained a position that nobody could challenge. It resulted from my ability to show a different face in every direction. While smiling angelically at the teacher, I was glaring at the child about to tell on me. The face on the right of my head asked for help from those who weren't yet sure of my guilt. Those on the left recoiled in fear, as my eyes stabbed thorns of future revenge deep into their pupils.

I stood there helpless between my many faces. Whenever visitors came to the house, I was happy again. I would sit in the living room with all the grown-ups and help Mum serve food and drinks. Mum and Dad tried to be happy, and for a brief moment the entire house was flooded in bright light.

House

Our house was built the traditional way, logs spaced slightly apart to let the air in. Happiness trickled away easily between the logs. After guests left, it was draughty for days. Mum cried and blamed everyone. Dad defended himself and tried to fix the house. He chopped up blocks of wood, but his hands were shaky, and the firewood wouldn't light; the side of the fireplace remained cold. The flues opened of their own accord and the wind came in via the oven's broken hatches and blew through every room in the house. Mum wrapped herself in shawls and turned blue with cold. She didn't have the strength to walk around the garden, which was warmed by the sun, but preferred to stay indoors, where it was chilly even in summer.

Dad stood on the riverbank casting a fishing line into the river until his hangover had subsided. That evening he smoked the fish he had caught and finally managed to light the stove beneath the sauna. Mum refused to take a sauna, and she only tasted a small piece of fish.

'Too salty. When will you learn?' she complained and turned away.

I was quite happy with salt and smoke. I tucked into the fish straight from the smoking tray and tried not to look at the innards dangling from the corner of Dad's mouth. Once the tray was empty, I dragged myself off to the sauna and threw water on the stove until I was sweating so much that I started to feel lighter. Dad opened the sauna door and squinted, but when I hollered at him he backed away and shut the door.

Dad puffed in the changing room until his beer bottle opened with a hiss and the sound of relieved burps edged their way through the wall. I caught them with the ladle and cast them on to the steaming stove, and soon the sauna was filled with the smell of freshly baked bread. I was hungry again. I wrapped myself in my dressing gown and walked through the changing room. Dad was sitting with his feet on the sofa, and cracked opened another bottle.

'Peeping Tom,' I hissed in unison with the bottle.

'Kristina, you're your Daddy's girl,' Mum bellowed from beneath the mountain of blankets.

I sliced up a loaf of white bread and spread the slices with lard. I stood there devouring the bread, and when Dad strode into the kitchen with a towel round his waist I might even have smiled at him.

'Don't let her be greedy,' came Mum's orders.

I handed Dad some of the slices of bread. He crammed them all into his mouth and washed them down with beer. His face swelled up. He reminded me of Aunt Miranda, who by the time she died was so fat that not even the burliest of the village men could carry the coffin from the church out to the cemetery. Miranda was a good person. She always fed me well. She would take my chubby face between her chubby hands and say:

'You've fair put on weight, girl.'

She said this meekly. Then she would lay the table and sit there watching me eat. She didn't let me leave the table until I had eaten more than I could manage, and she always looked sad if I refused to have any pudding. I could never bring myself to refuse her. I took a deep breath and filled my already overflowing stomach with baked cheese soaked in cream. To keep Miranda happy I finished up all the cloudberries too, though the seeds always got stuck between my teeth. After pudding I would eat a few chocolate sweets, each with a different filling, and I didn't say no when Miranda stuffed a whole bar of chocolate into my coat for the journey home.

The bar of chocolate disappeared as I walked home, as traipsing across the uneven fields created more space in my stomach. When Mum saw my stuffed face, she swore that one day she'd forbid me from ever stepping foot in Aunt Miranda's house again. We'd already stopped having meals together. Mum couldn't stand watching as Miranda filled Dad's glass to the brim with vodka and chuckled with satisfaction as he became more and more inebriated. Mum wanted to dictate what everybody drank. She politely avoided looking under the table, where the bottle Dad had chosen for himself stood propped against the leg of his chair.

Peace always had to be maintained, at least on Sundays. Or at least every other Sunday. Or at least once a month. Or at least at Christmas, some time, at least once in your life. Good God, at least once. Was that too much to ask?

Was it too much to ask that Miranda might have died on any day other than a Sunday, when the whole family was gathered together? But naturally, of all days, Miranda chose that day, thus ruining yet another day of domestic family bliss. Dad gathered the empty bottles into a plastic bag and ran across the fields to Miranda's cottage, then, once the ambulance had left, he ran down to the petrol station, and nobody knows where he ran from there. Mum didn't want to know. Bitterness flared up, as blistering as ever. He wouldn't even give her his sperm – his healthy sperm, that is! They had been too soaked in drink and vomit, and the babies just didn't have the strength to grow. They came out in a wash of blood, foetuses the size of mice. All seven of my siblings. But Mum had held me in by the force of her anger.

This anger had flowed into me, and with its strength I grew bigger and bigger, until Mum found it difficult to carry me. She cursed me too, but I just kept on growing; I would have grown to be a giant had I not been forcibly wrenched out with suction cups. Mum had wide hips, but the gate inside her hips was narrow. The gates to her heart were even narrower; I would never be thin enough to fit through them.

Pirta's mum came into the hallway. She wasn't invited any further inside the house.

'I want to talk about those lassies,' she said.

'What about them? Let them sort their own differences. They've got to learn.'

'Aye, you're right there.'

'I know I'm right.'

Mum shut the door. Pirta's mum walked backwards across the street. The door closed. The blinds were drawn. The cloak of darkness folded itself above Pirta's house too. The sun no longer tinged Pirta's freckles with copper red, and her face turned pale. Pessi stopped growing.

Mum wanted to help. She telephoned Pirta's mum and asked her to come over.

'What about hormone pills?' she suggested.

Pirta's mum pricked up her ears.

'It was the extra train, you know,' she muttered.

'He'll be back before long,' said Mum.

'He'll be back before long,' Pirta's mum repeated.

'Who's back? Is he on the train? Is he back yet?' shouted Pessi excitedly.

Both mums' ears tingled with awkwardness. Bright red balls of shame glowed on their cheeks. They returned to their respective houses. Their doors clicked shut. In the days that followed everyone came in and out by the back door. Mum crept out in her slippers, went to the hospital and came back the same way. Pirta's mum went via the train station to the petrol station, then on to the plastics factory, and from the plastics factory back to the petrol station, until they no longer needed her at the factory, and Pirta's supply of sticky-back plastic ran out. Her books had to make do without their coverings of red or yellow plastic. But it wasn't the covers her fingers wanted to scratch. Her fingers weren't searching for books. They were searching for skin and lips, blood and cigarettes.

Pirta didn't have to grow a fringe to cover her eyes. Nobody asked her anything, though she smiled through those pale, white lips. When Kari was around, nobody asked me either. The stink of the flats easily permeated your skin, and soon nobody wanted to come too close. A great barrier slowly formed around us.

Kari didn't look at people who jumped the queue in front of him and hissed nasty words at him through their clenched teeth. He looked at me and saw all my faults, my sagging stomach and my vagina that was far too tight. Within me there was no refuge for him. He escaped on his scooter, and while he was away I widened my vagina with a can of hair mousse. The surface of the bottle was cold and hard; it didn't give way. It vanquished the layers of tissue as they stretched and complained, but as the stretching came to an end my vagina seemed even tighter than before, didn't want to be touched, and drew its walls firmly together.

Strangers

Life in the flats was troubled, and it was the ancient Lapps' fault.

They used to camp there, and when they were kicked out of the village they placed a curse on the land: 'May he that builds here live to regret it.'

They didn't wreak their revenge on Old Pietu Vittikko, who oversaw the building work, but they regularly appeared to him. An angry Lappish man barged his way in Pietu's dreams and informed him that every dead Lapp would be summoned in front of the new house to cause a riot. The house would have to be built elsewhere or the residents would never have a moment's peace.

Pietu didn't believe his dreams. He saw the construction work through, and everything happened just as the old Lappish man had predicted. The residents were rowdy, and spread their madness throughout the village.

The Indians first made an appearance in Dad's dreams shortly after their arrival.

'We want some land,' they said.

Dad was sleeping off a hangover. He was afraid. It didn't occur to him to refuse their wishes.

'Town councillor's losing his mind,' said people around the village, as Dad started speaking on behalf of the Indians at council meetings.

The Indians were a group of young, long-haired people who had travelled by foot from France to Finland. Some of them were even related to one another. Others were only Indians in their heart of hearts. They wanted to see whether it was possible to live a natural life in the wilds of the northern forests.

They were beautiful. The men had long black hair that I wanted to clasp in my hands as they walked through the village towards Kittisvaara, where they were allowed to camp.

They built themselves tepees and set up house. After that nobody saw them for a long time. Nobody knew what they ate. The ground wouldn't yet yield any berries, and it was difficult to use frozen trees as nutrition.

Nobody knew. Not knowing makes you restless. Did they eat each other?

They stayed there all spring and all summer. Rarely did we see any of the long-haired people walking around the village. Those who did wander about were quiet and friendly; they would sneak down to the petrol station and polish off a few shifty pints. A number of the villagers visited their camp. We heard stories about them that made us even more restless. They slept during the day and stayed up all night, drank tea brewed from pine needles and didn't touch the roast reindeer that the council had offered them. They were happy with a dinner of bland vegetable soup and bread toasted on an open fire.

They were all far too thin.

Thankfully winter came early that year and the Indians were forced to ask for help. When the temperature dropped so much that they asked to be allowed to sleep in our houses, the community agreed to say no. For Mum this was easy; Dad would have been only too happy to accommodate one of their fiery-eyed women. Nonetheless, as the town councillor it was his job to inform the Indians that their tenancy had been terminated and that they were to continue on their way immediately.

After evicting the Indians, Dad drank solidly for two weeks. In the flats, the unrest grew. A young girl fell off the balcony – she didn't jump, she fell – and no one could say why. Her skull jangled merrily against the ground, though the people who came to collect her weren't laughing.

In my room I started playing Fainting and wished I could see the Indians again. It's difficult to press down on your own chest, but I managed to make myself unconscious by holding my breath after panting. They were walking over me. They wouldn't show me their faces, though I asked them to. They walked through walls, and when I tried to follow them the room began to spin. Doors locked all by themselves. I couldn't find my way out.

Once I'd finished panting I lay on the heaving floor. My eyes rolled about loose, until the end of my nose caught them and held them together. I stepped in through my nostrils and wound my way down the endless spiral staircases, and soon the Indians' scent was inside me. That same scent, familiar from the tracks. They walked through my mind and taught me to widen my gaze, and as the train approached they stepped on to the tracks, forcing the train to swerve to one side.

My mind and my eyes relaxed and I followed them along the riverbank. One foot moved in front of the other, but I was unaware of their movement. I simply walked onwards; I didn't focus my gaze because the Indians didn't either, and yet I could see everything, I could see the landscape moving, carrying us. I couldn't feel any motion within myself, yet a hand appeared from outside and reached through me again and again. A voice commanded me, disintegrating with the wind and turning into nothing but a soft murmur. It became part of a wall protecting me from all movement, just like the wail of the approaching sirens.

Kari had joined the crowd too, his eyes had relaxed and he had become a part of the moving landscape, and no one tried to stop him at the edge of the village. I alone had to stay behind, because I had to go to school the next day, had to open my eyes, straining until all the letters appeared on the right line, in the right order, leaning the right way. They leaned forwards or backwards, but not both ways at once as in the moving landscape. I couldn't hitch a ride into the forest that had swallowed Kari.

The Indians set up camp again, built their tepees and hauled heavy wet logs back to the bonfire. The council gave them an axe and some ready-chopped pieces of birch, which they burned at full moon in a secret ritual. It had been a mild winter. Early in the spring they were seen pulling nettle roots from the still-frozen earth, and when the sun finally thawed the ground they dug themselves trenches where they slept, covered only in spruce blankets until late in the autumn.

A sense of calm spread through the village. When the villagers fell asleep, the Indians rose from their trenches and turned the summer nights into brilliant light. Some said they had seen them dancing on the roofs of the houses in white robes. Others awoke to find an Indian sitting on the end of their bed, whiter than light. They mocked death; they never came to church, though the funeral bells clanged regularly. They didn't know how to cry. They didn't need to.

The village had a tender soul, one that was easily confused. It had to be protected from criminals and half-wits, from the mad teacher who had come up from the south and cycled up and down the village wearing shorts in temperatures of minus thirty and who drank milk straight out of the carton at the counter in the village shop. When he was invited up to the town hall for a little chat, he lay down on the table and started snoring, crushing Dad's new glasses. A thick darkness descended, making people bump into one another, until the teacher was sacked from his job, evicted and turfed out of the village; and only then did the air brighten up once again.

Weans

Pirta had a hunch.

'He'll be back before the winter,' she claimed.

'Don't kid yourself.'

'He said so.'

'Your dad's a liar.'

'Your dad sleeps around.'

'Let him.'

Dad walked into the room. 'Kristina, I've brought you a present.'

Pirta sniggered. 'A tart's present,' she cried and ran out of the room.

Dad cleared his throat. 'Pirta's father, you know . . .' he stammered as he held out the parcel.

'I know. Ran off to Oulu after another woman.'

'That's right, a *younger* woman.'

Dad spluttered as I tore open the wrapping paper. Inside the parcel, on a bed of velvet, lay a fountain pen.

'You don't read the way you used to. You don't like being alone,' he stammered.

The nib of the pen gently caressed the paper leaving beautiful, soft marks. I drew hearts and horses' heads. I sketched Kari's imposing features. All of a sudden, somebody grabbed me by the wrist.

'Dad, let go!' I shouted, but he had already left the room.

I could hear his coughing from beneath the floor.

My hand wrote by itself, filling the paper with letters I didn't recognise, forming sentences whose meaning I didn't understand. When the paper was full, my hand didn't stop writing at my command, but carried on writing across the tabletop. With my free hand I groped around the desk for more paper. When I ran out of space again, my hand continued writing on handkerchiefs and sanitary towels. Walls and wardrobe doors soon filled with letters. I climbed on to the table and let my hand write across the ceiling.

The door opened. Mum's weeping filled the room. The pen fell to the floor. I wet a flannel for Mum's eyes and scrubbed the room clean.

My tired hand began writing in letters that I knew.

That morning the sun didn't rise. I shaved the hair from my head and cycled to the market. The hangmen were already in place. Those about to be executed were standing in a row with black hoods covering their eyes. I climbed on to the podium and walked to the front of the row. The noose was wound around my neck before they had covered my eyes. I didn't wait to be pushed; I jumped. At that moment the sun rose and the hangmen realised their mistake. But I was already there, in the sun, and didn't know who I had been.

Dad read this and smiled.

'That's a fine story, lass. You're a realist.'

Once Dad had left I crawled into the floral tunnel

beneath my quilt. I lay on my back, rested my hands on my stomach, and commanded my muscles to relax. They responded by twitching violently. Someone grabbed hold of my wrist and forced my hand down into my trousers. My finger stroked the rough hair, caressed the small mound behind which colours became transfigured and a fresh breeze swept the wet moss from my lungs. When the sides of the abyss suddenly collapsed and sucked my finger inside with a wince, my hand wanted out again, up beneath the sky of flowers. It wanted to close my lips, which had opened too wide and let out a shrill cry of delight.

'What's the matter now?' asked Mum's sleepy voice from behind the door.

I burrowed under the blankets and held my breath until a sandstorm had blocked the path leading into the abyss and Mum's melancholy footsteps had faded into silence. My muscles recalled their soft pulse. Calmly they made space for my mind as it settled into the deepest, most beautiful regions of sleep.

Mum too visited those regions that night, and in the morning she was chirpy again as she sat leafing through an old newspaper.

'It's a sin. Some woman went and locked her weans in a toy box, and by morning they were dead,' she reported cheerily.

'That's nothing. Yesterday two weans were playing in the rubbish bin when the dustmen came round and scooped them into the cart. Got torn to pieces, they did,' Dad explained.

'The things you come up with.'

'It's all true.'

'Listen to this. There's a woman's shot her weans, then her man, then herself. She left the reindeer, mind.'

'Aye, so they can torment everybody else. She should've taken them with her.'

'Grandpa didn't shoot the reindeer.'

'Don't you start on about him. Grandpa was . . .'

'A good man,' Dad and I shouted in unison.

Dad patted me on the head.

'You know, Kristina, you're more like Grandpa than any of us.'

Jungle

The river flowed quietly by, its surface a mixture of all the most beautiful colours of the sky, colours which in Pirta's eyes found the shape and order of a rainbow. Pirta was walking in front of me, Aslak's love bites on her neck, throwing twigs and stones into the waves – even rubbish sometimes, if I didn't stop her in time.

'Get a life,' she quipped.

Pirta's narrow hips swung from side to side. Her hair glowed red in the sunlight. Her small breasts bounced gently beneath her thin shirt. I hunched my shoulders forward, trying to loosen the fabric of my jumper so that my breasts didn't look so full. If Kari had the choice, he would choose Pirta. She wasn't big and dark like me. But Aslak had got there first. Perhaps the river would reward Aslak, if I asked nicely; perhaps it would offer him a gentle way to die, many different ways.

The walk back to the village seemed to pass much more quickly when we thought up different ways of dying.

Pirta wanted to slit her wrists open, eat poisonous mushrooms or blow her brains out with a shotgun. I wanted to drown myself. Pirta wanted to slip a noose around her neck, jump in front of a lorry or overdose on sleeping pills. I wanted to drown myself. Pirta wanted to cover her head with a plastic bag, pass out in a snowdrift or rip her stomach open with a knife. I wanted to drown myself. Pirta wanted to starve to death, swallow razor blades or choke on vomit. I wanted to drown myself. Pirta was bored and wanted me to say something else, but the river was too close and forbade me. Only once we reached the village, far beyond the pull of the river, did I dare say:

'I'd drink a bottle of vodka and drive my dad's car into a tree.'

'You'd only end up paralysed and Kari would leave you.'

'Big fucking deal.'

We walked hand in hand past the town hall. The curtains in Dad's office had been drawn shut.

'Is that the car?' Pirta asked and pointed to a taxi parked outside the town hall.

'Give me a break,' I said, but by the time we reached the bingo hall I had regained my strength.

'Your mum's over there – in the front row,' I pointed out as Pirta quickened her step.

'Big fucking deal,' she mumbled without so much as glancing through the open doors at the monotonous mass of colours and numbers flooding from inside.

There was dog shit behind the supermarket. Hemppa's Caff was shut. We climbed up on to the roof of the bank. Pirta lit a cigarette and we smoked it in turns until we were both smeared with each other's lipstick and we both had stomach cramps. Up there we could smoke in peace. People walked past, their faces serious, their eyes fixed on the hot tarmac. No one looked up at the sky. The sun was too close; it had warmed too soon. The sun never asked whether it was okay to put in an appearance. Summer was a short, bright dream that no one dared believe until the air had chilled again.

That's when the cursing began:

'Great, another cold summer.'

And there was no end to it, even though there were still many hot days to come and the river boiled and haystacks raised on spears soon dried out, yellow in the heat.

'It's too dry. Won't be any mushrooms.'

And in the dark, damp forest summer grew stronger and stronger, carrying me through the winter, just as the river carried me towards the guileful spring. Pirta didn't need the river. She carried her flesh by herself, and her skin, heavy with warmth.

'D'you remember?' she asked.

'Of course.'

There was no need to say any more. There was no need to walk against the current, though both of us knew that the hill rising up behind the roofs wasn't just any old hill, nor were the trees on the hillside any old trees. Beneath their bark lay a smooth skin, something we had already lost. They belonged in the jungle, a place where we had played together in the knowledge that a hairy apeman was watching our every move. We imagined that, up in the trees, the hut our fathers had built would still be there, so our adventures wouldn't be interrupted by night or a hailstorm. The hut was very high up, hidden amongst the thick foliage. It was easy to climb up there along the tree's leaning trunk, but the apeman would always climb up the vines just as we were about to fall asleep. He would crawl inside the sleeping bag, offer us his hairy body, and his game refused to merge with the deep breath of sleep. He would hop along our shared skin and keep us awake until morning.

Now the apeman was alone. His sad eyes looked out across the roofs but he couldn't see us, because our faces were hidden behind a veil of grey smoke, and his hand couldn't break through the bark. The hut had been damaged during a storm. It needed some repairs, but our fathers didn't know anything about this and our hands weren't strong enough. My body refused to collect warming rays for itself; it stole heat from others, then shut off the smoke extractors too soon.

Scooter

The carbon monoxide fumes spread stealthily, odourless. Someone was battering my temples again. Mum was pacing from room to room opening the flues as quickly as Dad could shut them.

'Blue flames. You want to get us killed.'

'There's not so much as a spark. Look for yourself.'

Mum screwed up her eyes, groaned and grabbed her head with both her hands.

'Stop staring at me, I know I'm helpless.'

The village slowly revolved around the sun. The people all walked home along the bridge of light. The outer walls of the house dripped with sweat. Coals in the stove cooled and Mum complained of the cold.

Was it in the eyes?

The liver?

The brain?

In an old photograph, Grandpa looked serious, but his eyes were laughing.

'Fucking hell, Kristina, you've eyes like a spaniel,' said Kari.

It wasn't the eyes, then. We both had black hair. Grandpa's hair was speckled with white. I didn't have any grey hairs just yet. Would I ever have the chance to grow any if Grandpa compelled me to climb out on to the balcony? I wouldn't go on to the roof, not even if he tried to force me. The earth would have to turn on its side first, so that I'd climb up the railway tracks and open my mouth wide as the train hurtled out of the sky, and down into my intestines. In the photograph Grandpa was cut off at the waist; he had no large intestine, so he couldn't have cancer either. Grandpa escaped, he chose to jump before the disease had time to take root.

'Hold on,' Kari shouted and stamped on the accelerator.

The scooter bumped up and down along the tracks. My soft cushion of fat couldn't protect the base of my spine, which bounced painfully against the seat. Kari's sides were steaming. The sweat seeping through his shirt moistened my fingers, and I lost my grip. I was about to come crashing to the ground, when the oncoming train sounded its horn and Kari had to steer the scooter away from the tracks. We jolted along a bumpy forest path until we reached the main road. As our speed evened out, I leant against Kari's wet back and wrapped my arms tight around him.

'You're wet too,' he said as we stood outside the cottage.

We found an axe in the woodshed. I undressed while Kari smashed the lock. Naked, I stepped inside the cottage, into a room with no furniture save for a table and two long benches.

'Lie down over there. Hurry,' Kari instructed me.

My spine pressed sharply against the hard wooden table. I opened my legs, but at that very moment someone pushed them back together. Kari pulled down his shorts and lay on top of me. He dived back and forth with excitement. My legs opened. He entered me. He was softer than the can of mousse. He didn't have cold edges. My skin relaxed and the tissues yielded. Kari dived deeper. He swam with fast strokes until he reached the bottom, a region I had never managed to find. I shrieked with joy. I longed for him to stay, to crawl slowly along the bottom and gather up the finest shells and pebbles. But he was impatient. He exploded and went limp, withdrew, pulled up his shorts and ran outside.

The axe was left on the steps. I gathered my clothes from the yard, hurriedly pulled them on and ran after the scooter until Kari slowed down to let me clamber on.

Mum's triangular eyes glistened red in the lower corner of the window.

'Disappear, quick,' I shouted in Kari's ear.

The scooter shouted back as he revved on the accelerator. Behind the curtain Mum was straining her ears, but Kari didn't stop or drive away. He just stared ahead, the look in his eyes shredding the violets and petunias Mum had planted in the garden.

'Go, now,' I begged as another pair of eyes lit up in the window.

These new eyes were higher up; they were strong eyes. Not even Kari could resist their power. He kissed me with tightly pursed lips, pulled down his helmet and drove off.

'Who was that?' asked Dad.

'Nobody.'

'But has he finished school?'

'Yes, driving school.'

'For the love of God.'
'It was the last time.'
'You'd better promise it was the last time, or . . .'
'Of course it was. I promise.'

Resin

Somebody was constantly watching me. I couldn't even slip beneath the blankets by myself. When I danced around my room, cradling my tape player, Uncle's breath melted the frosted stars hanging on the windowpane. His breath rattled through my bedclothes as on sleepless nights I searched for a comfortable position. When I looked in the mirror, two black shadows moved behind me.

They didn't like the Sex Pistols. When I switched the tape off, the shadows disappeared, conjoined with one another in a single bright flash.

That's how I knew that Uncle had arrived. When I came downstairs, he was fidgeting on a kitchen stool, explaining in detail how many glasses of water he had drunk that day.

'Will you give your counting a rest,' Mum snapped.

She glared at him behind his back. Uncle saw this with the eyes he had in the back of his head, and left the room slamming the door behind him. I ran out after him.

'Make sure nobody sees you out with him,' Mum shouted.

'Your own brother! How can you say that?'

Uncle was bounding towards the road to Rovaniemi. His arms were flapping about like a pair of wings. Suddenly the fog wrapped itself around him and lifted him into the air. I tried to follow him, but I could hear Dad's voice shouting right in my ear, pulling me towards the ground.

'Take my word for it, lass, he's retarded.'

Uncle had disappeared. I slowly started walking back. One kilometre was equal to one burnt gram of doughnut. The rest swelled under my skin, forming ugly ridges beneath my chin, on my cheeks and buttocks. I would die of old age before I had burnt off all the doughnuts I'd ever eaten. If only I could shift old age; if I could stop breathing, jolt my brain, glare at my mind so that it fell from my body, then a light, floating spirit would be the only thing left of me. I wouldn't need to walk or move. The train would move me, carrying my limbs which it would crush beneath its belly, and blow hot air from its navel out over my scattered flesh. The world would melt; it would be fragrant.

As I walked, time disappeared, the years dissolved. I stepped into a ravine; abandoned watches drifted along its rim.

It was the resin that cured me, when in the sauna at Grandma's place I slipped on a bar of soap and fell against the red-hot stove. The skin on my arm caught on the side of the stove, and the sauna was filled with the smell of burnt fat. I ran outside and sank my arm into the deep snow. Back inside, Grandma wrapped my arm in a bandage smeared with resin. Beneath the bandage my skin was alive. It festered and stank, but the resin prevented it from becoming inflamed. It revived my cells, allowing the skin to grow again. Afterwards there wasn't the slightest mark.

Not on my skin.

I didn't take a sauna with Uncle, though Grandma told me to. I went in by myself and threw lots of water on the stove. The glass in the window was old and warped. Outside the yard heaved, and as the window steamed up everything turned into a nettle-scented dream that swallowed me up and carried me into Grandma's cottage. There they sat in a row on the sofa, Grandma, Grandpa and Uncle, all staring at the television screen. Grandma and Grandpa were in their dressing gowns, while Uncle had only a towel tied around his waist. They stared at the screen, Grandma and Grandpa all serious, Uncle giggling hysterically. The dog's long tongue wound its way in between his toes, licking them each in turn, then made its way up his legs until it reached the thin hair on his head and the hairs sprouting from his ears, and Uncle's giggling soon drowned out the sound of the television altogether. Grandpa only had to bellow at them once; the giggling stopped abruptly and Uncle slunk off to his room, the dog following close behind him.

I sat there in silence, sniffing at the scent of tar on my skin. My eyes stared at the television, but they didn't see a thing. Neither did Grandma's eyes, as snores rattled through her body. Grandpa looked at me apologetically, but didn't say anything. I didn't want to talk either. I was glad that Uncle had gone, and that I no longer had to constantly shoo the dog. One lick would have been enough to contaminate my sauna-clean skin.

Talons

I had a dream that an old Lappish man appeared, ripped off Dad's testicles with his teeth and singed a mark into Mum's ear. As for me, he dragged me outside and thrust a red-hot iron between my legs. By morning the man had gone, Mum was chirpy and Dad apparently still had his testicles intact; I caught a pungent whiff of cologne as he hurried out of the door. The only mark left was on me. A glowing red circle where once my pubic hair had flourished. My skin smelt burnt. I no longer felt the urge to stick my hand down my trousers in search of the tingling path leading into the abyss. I didn't want to be alone under the blankets – especially at night, as the itching started earlier and earlier.

The itch had a life of its own. During the day it was calm, but as evening drew in so the restlessness began. It was asleep, then awake; awake, then asleep. It wandered wherever it wanted, cackling and mocking me. When I was awake I would lie in silence listening to its insults. During my sleep I would reveal my eagle's talons and attack it.

There are two kinds of pain: honest pain and sly pain. Honest pain is when you're standing by the edge of the ice rink and a puck flies up towards your unprotected face, breaking your nose before spinning back to Kari, who thwacks it at Aslak. Instead of getting out of the way, Aslak skates right at the puck and hits it right into the goal, by which time I'm already in hospital with a heavy bandage over my nose, my painkillers ingested, and gradually the pain dies down. That's honest pain. It fades and grows, fades and grows, fades and fades and fades and dies away altogether and never comes back, because the game's up, the ice rink is melted, and there won't be another winter with Kari or a reason to go back down to the rink and freeze.

The itch, however, never stops. That's because it's sly. At first it feels good. It charms you and seduces you. It sings sweetly, its voice full of clear, bright overtones, until you're forced to give in, and under the protective gauze of sleep softly press your nails into the skin and scratch and scratch, and only then does it remove the mask to reveal its scabby face.

You could cut off your hands. Then you wouldn't be able to scratch.

Adolf Korteniemi lost his hands by accident.

Adolf left for Norway without asking permission, landed a job at a fish factory, and once when he was cleaning the cutting machine someone accidentally switched it on and his hands were sliced to pieces. When Adolf came home, the petrol station lifted its ban on him and started putting a straw in his pint glass.

Handless Adolf was always smiling. Before his accident he would walk around with a scowl on his face, never waving at passers-by like everybody else did. Everybody said hello, everybody knew everybody else and said hello to them, but Adolf only became all right after losing his hands.

'You're crazy,' said Kari.

But he still took me into the woods when I asked him. He turned off the scooter's engine and stared at the ground as I undressed and climbed up into a tree. With the axe I cut an open wound in the bark and straddled the tree, positioning the sore area over the spot where resin began to seep from the wood. The tree healed itself, and I didn't cut any new wounds in it. The tree healed me too, though only for a few hours, because it was almost night and my nails had started to grow again.

Family outing

Mum was packing a bag.

'A change of scenery will do a world of good,' she said.

Dad was dancing around in his slacks.

'Don't hurry back, eh!'

I put velvet sheets on my bed. Once Dad had disappeared I'd invite Kari round. Through the front door.

'You can keep your Mum company,' Dad declared.

In the mirror I could see my skin darkening before me as I scrubbed away my disappointment with soap. Once on the bus, my face tingled and stung. The green landscape poured through the window and Mum drifted into sleep. She only woke up when I pinched her bony arm as we approached the stop by Grandma's cottage. She took a bottle of pills from her handbag and looked around furtively, and, although there was no one on the bus but us, she decided to place the bottle back in her bag.

Uncle was sitting in an armchair in front of the television, his hand deep inside his underpants, wanking.

'Give that a rest – a grown man!' Grandma ordered him.

The hand stopped still. His mouth gave a low growl. I petted the dog that lay at Uncle's feet, and sniggered as its tail wagged gaily back and forth across my face. Uncle sniggered too and removed his hand from his underpants. Grandma returned to the kitchen and resumed mashing the potatoes. She smiled at me from behind Uncle's armchair. She couldn't see that the hand had slipped back inside his underpants and was moving rhythmically again.

That evening the bedroom door wouldn't stay shut. Uncle rocked in his armchair, his eyes bulging out of their sockets. They glowered through the hinges in search of a way into my bed. I only went to bed once Mum had come back from the woods. Grandma had laid a couple of mattresses out on the floor. The sheets and blankets were light as clouds. They were waiting for night, so they could billow up into the sky with our dreams. I undressed slowly, but when the door gave a creak I pulled my tights back on and put on a long-sleeved nightdress.

Mum put on one of Grandma's flannel nightshirts, smoothed some cream over her face to rejuvenate her skin, and disappeared beneath the mountain of blankets. I beckoned sleep and prayed that during the night it might blow Mum further away too, that the bed would divide in two. That the two parts would slip in different directions, each to their respective walls.

Once Mum had fallen asleep, the mattress opened up to reveal a ravine, and we began to fall. The oily straw prevented us from breathing.

It was a long time before morning came and drove Mum back out to the woods.

Grandma bellowed at Uncle, who was already wanking in his armchair. Then she lifted an enormous pot on to the stove and sent me out to fetch firewood.

The woodshed was at the far end of the barn. The cold stone floor numbed the soles of my bare feet. I quickly hopped between piles of stinking dung and hurled blocks of wood into the basket until it was full. Nobody had cleaned the barn since the cows had moved away. Terrified shivers ran down my spine as, from beneath the floor, I could hear the sound of lowing. It wouldn't stop, though I started singing at the top of my voice.

'That's not a cow. That's old Harald Niva moaning again,' Grandma tried to comfort me.

She sat down on the bench and began telling me the story, though I told her I'd heard it before.

That it was Harald who used to drive Finnish terrorists across the border into Sweden.

That it was Grandpa who finally turned Harald in, and because he was a miserly man, only took part in Harald's slaughter for a small fee.

That the cows were lowing like there was no tomorrow, but that only one word came out of Harald's mouth:

'Grass.'

After repeating the word several times, Grandma burst into tears.

'No matter, he was a good man.'

'Harald?'

'Your Grandpa.'

'Right.'

'Just like your Daddy.'

'Right.'

'And as for you . . . Aye, you're a good lassie. Your Daddy's girl.'

'And Grandpa's girl too.'

'A bloody good man!' Mum cried.

She stepped into the cottage once Uncle had got dressed and walked out the door. Grandma blocked her ears and sang hymns while Mum hoovered the dog-hair from the sofa and shouted above the noise that some of her hair must still be on the floor too. Grandma used to pull her children by the hair whenever they tried to get into the pantry. They were forced to eat leftovers and beg for food in their own home, because Grandpa never came home for at least a week after each payday.

'A good man, indeed,' Mum repeated, this time slightly more subdued.

She soon emptied her bottle of pills, and before long we were sitting on the bus on the way home. Dad met us at the bus stop in the car.

He gave a stiff smile. Mum sat in the back seat, her eyes fixed ahead. I sat in the front and let Mum's pupils bore their way through the skin on my neck.

As he drove, Dad cracked open a bottle, and a deluge of words came out of Mum's mouth.

'A bloody good man. He was a good-for-nothing just like you. My Mammy used to sleep in her boots, you know, didn't have the strength to take them off in the evenings. She'd just collapse on her bed, then get up again and go straight out to that cowshed. I tried talking to my Pappy. Work's killing her, I said. He just patted me on the head, looked me in the eyes with that smirk on his face and says, so it is. And it's a good job too.'

'Not my fault, is it.'

'Don't you start, you devil! Your Mammy never cleaned in her life. She'd just sit on a stone in the garden, her eyes blank while I scrubbed that house, from the loft right down to the cellar, damn it. Let me tell you, nobody'd ever cleaned those steps. They hadn't! There was mould on the damned things!'

'You're calling your own daughter a devil?'

'I don't have to. Look in front of you, man. There's one right there in the middle of the road.'

'Bloody hell!'

The car started to swerve. Dad pulled in at the side of the road and told me to get in the driver's seat.

'Don't you worry about your Mammy,' he said and polished off his bottle.

Mum whimpered the rest of the journey.

'Keep your heads down,' she stammered just before we turned into the yard.

I hunched across the steering wheel and drove past the windows that opened on to the road like great, curious eyes. The garage swallowed us up before anyone could call the police. We dashed inside in a line, like burglars. In the hallway Doughnut was running around in hysterical circles and dashed out between Dad's legs. Dad dashed out behind him and didn't come back.

Alina

As evening drew in, Doughnut was shoved out of the taxi and into the yard. I let him inside and he whined with exhaustion, but Mum showed no sign of comforting him, choosing instead to pelt him with raw potatoes.

'What did you see? Say something before I wring your neck,' she howled.

I ran into the kennel after Doughnut. The night was cool, but I didn't feel it. I wrapped a blanket round my head so that nobody could see that Doughnut wasn't alone in his bed. I slept heavily, and when the sun began to warm me the following morning I crept inside for something to eat. Mum was sitting at the kitchen table.

'Your father's not come home.'

I called Doughnut inside.

Don't be afraid, she's calmed down, my eyes tried to tell him, and I wrapped my arms around Mum's shoulders.

I ran my hands through her hair, rubbed her tense scalp with my fingers. I stroked the skin around her eyes and hummed a lullaby until she finally relaxed.

'Be strong for me, Kristina,' she implored.

A sandwich had dried out and shrivelled on the table. Beneath my arms Mum shrunk and curled up. I removed the plate and walked into my room. Mum came after me, whimpering.

'Take him these,' she said, handing me Dad's fur hat and a pair of mittens.

'Mum, it's warm outside.'

'Kristina.'

'I don't want to.'

'Kristina.'

Her words dripped heavily. I didn't have the strength to push them aside. I walked Doughnut down to the petrol station. I dived in through the fug of thick grey smoke, walked up to Dad's table and hit him with the hat and mittens.

'Mum says hello,' I shouted above the guffaws.

There was a taxi in the forecourt; a fat woman was sitting in the driver's seat, her lips spilling worried-looking smoke rings out through the open window. The same woman Kari had seen kissing Dad in the television room over at the flats. The same woman I had seen writhing beneath Dad when I had secretly peered through the window at the cottage. The same woman.

The woman.

The woman whose scent whipped Mum's voice into a piercing siren.

The woman.

Fatally attractive. Alina.

Her name was never breathed in our house.

'What state was your Pappy in?' Alina asked.

I stepped through one of the smoke rings and it carried

me far away, to a beach where Pirta and Aslak were lying on a large towel, their limbs wrapped around one another. Surrounding them was an open, empty space dotted around the edges with wicked pairs of eyes. I sat down on the edge of the towel and rolled up my trouser-legs and the ends of my sleeves, damp with sweat.

'Kari's gone. He was tired of waiting,' Aslak informed me.

I stepped into the changing cabin and took off my clothes. My bikini bottoms were tight and tufts of hair curled out around the edges. My breasts wouldn't stay inside the tiny upper half. I sat on the bench for a moment, took off my bikini and put my sweaty clothes back on.

'You're taking your time. Let us in!' shouted Pirta.

I took off my clothes again and put on my bikini. I wrapped a towel around myself and stepped out of the cabin. Aslak stared at me with clouded eyes. His mohican had flopped down across his face. My eyes moved across his milk-white body and stopped at his shiny pink swimming trunks. Nausea rose from the bottom of my stomach. I escaped into the cool undercurrent of the river.

Rays of sunshine pierced the surface of the water and refracted into thousands of golden flowers.

'That was a brave thing to do,' said Kari's voice within me.

My hairs and my hips disappeared. I held my breath for a long time. Then I opened my mouth and embraced a whirlpool which smashed the light-flowers and sprayed my eyes with white mist. Nearby was a sunken ship full of treasure, a forsaken death that wanted to show me its powers. I opened myself up to the flowers, I became the whirlpool, and I was just about to let go when the roar of a motor tore my dream apart, and with urgent strokes I thrashed up to the surface.

I fell back into the water's embrace. It accepted me, caressed my back and gently rocked me. Alina turned off the motor and reached out her hand. Pairs of translucent hands reached out to support Dad as he saw me, burst into tears and tried to peer over the side of the boat.

'No, sit!' Alina barked.

The shimmering hands climbed back up into the sky.

Tent

I swam backstroke to the shore, walked up to my towel and lay down. Pirta's giggling could be heard from the changing cabin. I pressed my tongue firmly against the top of my palate and let the sun's hot tongue press my body against the rough earth.

I spent the whole summer there and wished that nothing would ever change. That my bikini top wouldn't seem any smaller and that my trousers wouldn't split at the seams.

I wished that the whirlwind would gather its strength and whirl away backwards. It would be summer before then, like all those summers before Aslak existed, when Pirta was allowed to stay at Nan's too.

We would sit on the back seat giggling, our lips covered in syrup, Dad's face beaming in the rear-view mirror. He put up a great big tent in Nan's back yard. There was plenty of room in there for us to jump up and down, and once the long zip had been done up in the evenings we used to play Mummies and Daddies. Pirta had short hair, so she was the boy and lay on top of my naked body. She got to kiss me with her hard lips tightly squeezed together, and I got to moan the way I imagined grown-up women do.

Pirta's bony body felt safe inside the sleeping bag. I shaped her into a nest for myself, a place where bad dreams couldn't find me and where, in the morning when I awoke in the orange glow of the tent, I dared to be happy about the warm day ahead which would take us to the water and back, again and again. I never tired of looking at my reflection in the sauna mirror. Black hair spilled down, wet around my shoulders. My face was pale and in my eyes there glimmered an emerald I had borrowed from Pirta. My breasts swelled prettily as I breathed in. I was Brooke Shields at the Blue Lagoon. Pirta was my red-haired, freckled husband.

Hand in hand we wandered through this island paradise and I worshipped the sun as its caresses turned our skin brown, made fruit grow larger and juicier so that when we shook a tree hunger and fatigue disappeared in an instant. We were happy and content until the sun removed its smug mask and stuck out its tongue, darkening the sky, slithering around the world like a translucent snake captured inside a shimmering aura.

'I'm not your boyfriend anymore,' Pirta snapped.

Autumn appeared before she could finish that nasty sentence. Autumn appeared and knocked over the tent, tore the dresses from around the trees and commanded the naked trunks to kneel before the might of the northern winds. They had laid their spindly limbs across the path as I walked from the primary school to the secondary school and hid in the toilet. As I took comfort by a lukewarm radiator a wet filter was thrust between my lips; as fear disappeared out the back door, I dared to inhale the bitter smoke deep, deep down to where my roots fumbled in search of fertile ground. As the playground assistant stepped into the toilet, I hid behind my fringe and faded my body into invisibility.

Dad held a meeting in honour of which the sound on the television was turned off and Mum demanded that I comb my fringe to the side. They examined the list of people in my class and read out the names of those people I ought to associate myself with. Mum decided that Raija, the bank manager's daughter, would be a good friend for me, and that for a boyfriend I could have Petteri, whose father was the headmaster.

'No lads for you yet,' Dad growled.

A star appeared by the names of acceptable friends. Neutral names were marked with only a line, while those with whom I should never be seen were marked with skulls. Kari wasn't in my class, but on this list he had a column all of his own, full of skulls.

'Don't you put a foot inside that slum,' Mum warned me.

Dad cleared his throat. I gave my head a shake, letting my fringe darken the world, while Dad turned the sound back up on the television.

Canister

We lay on the tracks, our cheeks against the cool steel, our bodies, warm and alive, side to side next to one another. We lay on the tracks, and the earth's tremors made our hearts race to an almost stifling rhythm, until just before it was time to jump on to the verge, out of the path of the sparking, oncoming train.

Once the train had passed we rolled about, without a thought for the sharp edges of the stones on the ground. We rolled about, our hair and faces covered in sand and dust, and kissed each other, the bitter taste of tobacco on our lips and tongues, and we didn't spare a thought for the coming evening, the coming night or morning, knowing that we could never speak of this, that no words could ever reveal what it was like to be hurled into a wild dance with death.

This was better than idleness. Some people sensed death, ran up to the gates, jumped on its back and rode away without saying goodbye.

Like Oula.

I had known him too. He lived on in a crumpled photograph in Aslak's back pocket and never stopped smiling.

'I'm coming with you, brother,' Aslak promised, but didn't smile.

He still blamed himself, and not even Pirta could console him. He had invoked death, and when it finally arrived he was asleep and Oula had gone instead.

'Don't go,' his mum had pleaded, but death had made its mind up.

It lit a fire in Oula's eyes that burned their mother's pleas to a cinder.

'Please yourself then,' she had said, and Oula got into the car.

The fishing lines and equipment had been packed in the boot. Oula squeezed into the car that drove down to the riverside, and joined a group of people who didn't know the river's mind. He knew that he shouldn't, but death pushed him back, gently helped him into the boat, then dived under the water where it lay in wait. The fish died in vain. Their thrashing bodies were hurled back into the water as the boat capsized and the strong current of the rapids pulled Oula's trousers down around his ankles. He couldn't swim. A whirlpool pulled him inside, drew him beneath the surface and killed him. The others held on to the upturned boat. They were saved. One of them reached out, grabbed Oula's hand and tried to save him, but the current was too strong. He had to let go; Oula had to be released.

At the very moment Oula died, Aslak woke up and saw that his big brother's cherished paintings had fallen from the wall. Their frames had broken. Blood seeped through the cracks, confusing the colours. Aslak's eyes flooded. As there came a battering at the door, he already knew that Oula had gone, leaving him alone to a summer that was too bright, stopped him sleeping, and stopped him speaking after Oula's rubber boot was washed ashore; they never found his body, though the whole village helped dredge the river.

Aslak lay awake, battling with his own thoughts which darkened with every passing autumn, until Kari knocked on his window and beckoned him out into the world, down to the railway tracks, whose trembling demands he could already feel in his chest.

His big brother had been courageous. Why couldn't he be too?

'You can do it, but don't go without me,' asked Pirta.

'I'll go if I like,' Aslak snapped and disappeared into the woods.

'Don't go,' she begged him.

She walked behind Aslak and shrunk. She was a little girl, small enough to slip out between her mother's legs and into the hallway when the door opened and her uncle walked in.

'Dad's cleaning his rifle,' she exclaimed, but her uncle was already on his way out; Pirta grabbed hold of his trouser legs and hung on by her teeth and fingers, and her uncle laughed.

Laughter bubbled from her father's mouth too. He stood up to greet her uncle, but then somebody shouted, there was a terrible bang, and suddenly the laughter dripped from her uncle's mouth in black clots of blood as he lay on the floor, his cheek hanging off, and Pirta wasn't sure whether the bang came first then the shout, or the shout first, or what had happened, and the laughter in her father's face had died and his eyes frozen.

'I tackled him, Dad. But not on purpose,' Pirta cried.

She ran away from her father's grey face. She ran far

away, until a firm pair of hands took hold of her and took her even further away, to some other village, and when she was finally brought home again everything was new. The rug, the curtains, the sofa and her father lying there, his mouth only rarely opening to let out a laugh.

Laughter had been replaced by the pealing of funeral bells. They hammered out the same rhythm as the bells in Aslak's head. They latched on to one another and for a fleeting moment the sound quietened and turned into a beautiful melody. Kari heard it too, but Pirta was already taken and he decided to fall in love with me instead.

Only at night did the terror come, once the train had come careering through our dreams, reflecting against the wall the severed limbs, the brains running in a thin trickle down the verge, that strange, black power, all-consuming and torturous. There was no room for light in the picture, nor for the comfort or defiance of day. It was a black picture that grew in our minds, forcing us to do things again and again, to wait just a second or two more before diving back into life's tepid embrace.

After the train had passed we ran along the tracks to the railway bridge, where Kari and Aslak were celebrating at the other side. They had run across the bridge and jumped on to the verge as the train was already caressing their backs. It was a record, and to honour this they drank home-brew and planned their next stunt.

'I'm going to lie on the tracks and let the train drive over me.'

'You'll get yourself killed.'

'So fucking what?'

'I'm coming too,' I said.

'You? You're way too fat. The train'll be derailed!'

Excitement stiffened in my throat. I sucked in my stomach until it was an aching hollow. Nobody would see it – ever again. But Kari's devilish eyes were unrelenting. They rolled up the hem of my jumper, and I held my breath so that my tummy wouldn't flop into view.

Aslak was kissing Pirta. Kari sat down next to me and wrapped his bony arms around me. I looked at his legs in silence. They were scrawny, like thin sticks, at least three times narrower than my thighs. Sitting next to me he looked like a skeleton draped with clothes.

'Come here,' he whispered.

Kari rose into the air when I jumped off him. I reached my hand out to Pirta, who had extricated herself from Aslak's arms. We ran across the tracks and into the woods, where Pirta placed her warm lips against my neck and bit hard.

'That's what he did, just like an animal,' she whispered and stuck out her tongue, blood swelling from its tip.

The door into Mum's room was open, and the indentation in the bed empty. The medicine cabinet also gaped empty. She had left a note on the table saying that she'd gone to work.

Fear gripped my hand; it disappeared in between my legs, into the abyss. I was afraid that the pain would stop and wouldn't flow out through my fingertips after all. When crystal vases and porcelain birds started flying against the walls, I ran down to the cellar to look for sausages and carrots to help me explode. I couldn't stop the explosions, though knives and forks and heavy pieces of furniture were hurtling towards me. When a frying pan struck me on the forehead I lay immobile for a long time and a deep silence filled the house. An invisible statue was placed in front of my bedroom door, and I couldn't squeeze my way past it until I heard the slam of the front door and the strains of Dad's drunken singing.

During R.E. I told Birgitta about the flying objects.

'It'll be the devil raging. He'll be back soon with his seven cousins,' she explained.

I stood outside the house and tried to decide which doors the cousins would use.

The blinds had been pulled down. Mum had just come back from night shift and she'd be asleep for the next two months. I put my schoolbag on the steps and walked across the road to Pirta's house. Pessi was sitting in front of the television staring at the black screen.

'I miss Dad,' he said.

'Give us a cigarette, a real one,' I demanded.

'I've stopped smoking. The school's full of police these days.'

I proferred a tub of chewing tobacco I'd stolen from Lennart's shop on the Swedish side. He quickly rolled himself a stinking ball of the stuff and stuck it beneath his upper lip.

As we walked into the woods, invisible hands twisted themselves around me and squeezed me hard. A large rock appeared before me. Pirta was sitting on top of it. When he saw her, Pessi burst into tearful whimpers.

'She'll beat me up. Mum said she's allowed to,' he sobbed, spitting black snot into the moss.

But Pirta wasn't angry.

'Amazing,' she sighed and handed him the canister.

Her smile stretched wide as the landscape. Pessi took a sniff and launched into flight. The canister breathed enticingly and there was nothing I could do but sniff its moist lips. My head felt light as my brain flowed out with my breath. When I breathed in, my breasts contracted. I pressed my fingers into them and listened to the sound, as my spirit sizzled down into my stomach, ruffled its wings and flew off after Pessi.

'Fuck, that's amazing!'

The canister grew a pair of legs and ran into hiding. Crawling along the ground, I tried to catch it. My teeth moved in their gums. My face crumpled.

'You look like an old biddy,' Pirta giggled as she opened the lid.

I crawled up to the coffin and peered inside. There I lay. My spirit was inside the canister, which had now risen high into the air. I shouted for help and Uncle appeared. He reached out his hand, yanked me out of the coffin and dragged me over to the canister. I sniffed and sniffed. My nostrils widened and split with a joy that lulled me to sleep.

The rock was deserted. The skin on my face had peeled off, my plastic-smelling brain melted fast into the rock. Petrol streamed from my eyes. Trees stretched their naked branches out towards me, their fingertips glistening with Uncle's mischievous thoughts. Pirta and Pessi had disappeared and taken the coffin with them. Pessi's baseball cap lay on the ground. Inside it, a chalk-white reindeer skulled wheezed:

'Away back home!'

I opened one door, then another. Cracks appeared in the floor, and trying to avoid them I staggered back to the staircase. Mum staggered in front of me.

'My head hurts,' I whined.

'You've probably got a migraine too – at your age!'

I groped for a tablet from the bottle and swallowed it

with some difficulty.

'I think I'll join you,' Mum sighed and popped a handful of pills into her mouth.

At midnight, after the train had passed, sleep came and hurled me to the floor. A hole appeared in the ceiling; petrol seeped through. I tried lying on my side. A sneering man crawled out from beneath the bed. I turned on to my back. Men swam above me in a line. Their genitals brushed against my sweaty face. Their bottomless pupils swallowed my eyes. I pulled the sheets over my head and died. As I revived, a man rose from beneath the bed holding out a burning torch.

'Mum, Mum!'

The man disappeared.

'What's the matter? You're a big girl now,' Mum whispered, stroking my hair.

'They've pissed the bed, and I'm all wet.'

'Wake up, lass, wake up.'

My limbs numb, I lay in the fresh sheets Mum had put on the bed. I lay there for one day and one night, and only then did a great tongue appear and gently press me deep into a mattress filled with dreams.

'Don't you tell anybody about it,' Mum made me promise.

I told Kari.

'Fucking nutter.'

I told Pirta.

'Fucking amazing.'

I told Birgitta during our psychology class.

'Of course, we can't deny that some of us are simply possessed,' she proclaimed, and the class exploded into fits of laughter.

Woods

Mum was sitting at the piano. Beneath the minor tones you could just make out the calming tap of sharply filed, carefully lacquered fingernails as they struck the keys. Tears turned Mum's eyes into a dark blue ocean where I let myself drift on the crests of waves.

'Dad, come and join us,' I shouted, but he was already cycling towards the village, his thoughts already sinking into the arms of a busty woman.

'But why ugly Alina? Why not pretty Mum?'

'It's because she drives him around,' Mum explained.

Pirta didn't buy this explanation.

'Your dad's an old whoremonger,' she said bluntly.

I tried to defend him. 'They just drive around together.'

'Yeah right,' she scoffed and beckoned for Pessi to come into the room.

'Pessi, tell Kristina where you saw her dad with the taxi driver.'

'Coming out of the hay shed.'

'And you saw them with your own eyes?'

'Yes.'

'See, I told you,' Pirta snapped and pushed Pessi to the floor.

'Mum! Pirta's bullying me!' he screamed.

Nobody replied. The house was quiet and deserted. Pirta lay on her bed swallowing her tears. From the other room we could hear Pessi's sobs, interspersed with bursts of rage and shouting.

'Fucking bitch! Fucking bitch!' he shouted and kicked the wall.

'Go and slap him,' Pirta muttered.

I went into the living room and stuck a video in the player. Pessi threw himself into an armchair.

'Roll us a smoke,' he asked.

I tore a page out of the newspaper, rolled it up and lit the end. Bitter smoke burned my eyes and lungs. Dad and that woman were lying in the hay shed kissing. Dad was lying on top of her, her skirt hitched up. I handed Pessi the roll of paper and escaped into the screen.

The woods are fresh and kind. I follow the others carrying a large picnic basket. I feel light and happy. It's already evening as we arrive at the house. We light the fire and start making supper. It's lots of fun, but at the stroke of midnight the house spits the burning logs out on to the floor, and we have to escape. It's not fun any longer. We run out into the woods. Outside it's dark and stormy. The path is blocked with fallen tree trunks. It's hard to get past them. We stagger onwards. Someone cries out. Christine is lying on the ground. The trees' roots twist around her legs, pulling them apart. A thick log comes hurtling through the darkness and flies right through Christine. All of a sudden it's morning. Christine is nowhere to be seen, but the forest is crying out, and it has Christine's voice.

The television screen darkened. The room had filled with thick smoke. Pessi was coughing and snivelling. I opened a window and tried to fan away the images of Dad's rosy backside and that woman's jiggling breasts. I took Pessi in my arms and squeezed the fear out of him, and soon he rested his arm round my neck and took me with him into a world of dreams.

Taxi

Uncle raced ahead without looking to the side. I peddled after him, shouting at him to slow down, to answer me, how many more days, how many hours before we die.

Uncle didn't stop. He raced ahead, his eyes fixed on the woods. He didn't so much as glance at me, nor at the puzzled faces of people in passing cars. I jumped off my bike and shoved it into the woods, then walked off briskly along the main road. I waved my hands in just the same way as Uncle. When a taxi pulled up next to me and its back door opened, I couldn't resist. I hopped in, though the day's calories were far from burnt off.

Alina slammed her foot on the accelerator. My thoughts melted into the landscape and disappeared as we built up speed.

'We're going to die together, Kristina. Just you and me.'

'Why?'

'You don't want to help me.'

'What do you want?'

'Talk to him. Tell him to leave your Mammy.'

'Okay.'

'Promise?' Alina shouted and let go of the steering wheel.

Back home Dad's eyes followed my every movement from behind his newspaper.

Don't you blab to your mother, they said.

I went and stood in front of the television.

'Stop hitting Doughnut.'

Dad's body twisted like an angry snake.

'Out the way, damn it,' he yelled.

'Stop hitting Doughnut.'

'Damn it.'

Dad strode out into the yard and picked up the shovel, though no new snow had fallen for several days. I became light and rode on his shoulders as the mountains of snow moved from one place to another. Every now and then I dived head first into the snow and burrowed my way into a glowing tunnel which Dad had dug out especially for me. When I came out the other end of the tunnel I was big again and Dad couldn't carry me. My flesh was heavier than wet snow and Dad's muscles had wasted away.

'Has he lost his mind?' Mum despaired as Dad's shovel reached the sand beneath the snow.

'Aye, barking mad,' Dad replied as he came back inside, and threw me a mean glance.

He lay down on the sofa and switched on the television. When the telephone rang he turned the volume up even further.

'Nobody answer,' he said firmly, and Mum rushed over to the medicine cabinet.

Later in the evening Doughnut started to howl. Dad nodded when I looked at him unflinchingly, and I dared to fetch the dog inside. Dad didn't say anything when I lifted Doughnut with me up into the armchair and stroked his cold paws. On the television there was a programme about girls who refused to eat. They were sick, sick in the head, Dad said, as the girls clambered out of the screen and into his arms.

'Yuck!' he muttered, but his voice was brimming with tenderness.

I touched my body. Lots of fat and sagging skin, bones deep inside. I had a long way yet to reach Dad's arms.

Teeth

The telephone didn't ring again. Dad slumped deeper into the sofa.

Objects started moving by themselves.

When I went to sleep, I never knew where I would wake up in the morning. Sometimes my bed was against the wrong wall, and sometimes it was even in the wrong room.

Mum agonised and was endlessly looking for her things.

'Your mother's demented,' Dad claimed.

'Your mother's demented,' he claimed when his own things went missing too.

'Demented old cow!' he would snap, hunting after his glasses.

Mum didn't wake up to answer him. She was asleep for the seventh day in a row, and Dad sank to the floor, out of breath. Only then did his glasses slowly drift towards him and position themselves in front of his eyes. He could *see* me.

'Bring me my teeth!' he spluttered.

They were on his bedside table, floating in a glass of yellowish liquid. I imagined an axe cutting through the air again and again, trying to crush Grandad as he yanked the healthy teeth from Dad's mouth. His friends were given shotguns and fishing equipment as confirmation presents; the children of church-goers were given golden crosses. Dad got a set of false teeth, the first in the village. He tried to refuse as best he could, but when he opened his mouth his jaws locked into place, and by the time the lock opened again the dentist had already finished.

Once his new teeth were in place it was easier for Dad to join in the family mantra:

'Pappy was a good man, the best of men, a good man, the best of men.'

Faces

Time tangled itself up. Hunger reeked havoc in my mouth, making my teeth fragile and translucent. When Mum told me to eat something, I escaped and went to Pirta's place. A few drops of acetone on a tissue were enough to dispel the hunger. The smell spread beneath the door and through the house, and Pirta's mum didn't ask me up to the table.

'Bloody kids!' she screamed.

'Give it a rest, Mum,' peeped Pessi.

'Out of here, the lot of you! Kristina too. Or do you want me to get on the phone to your fancy father?'

'If she rings, don't listen to her. She's not right in the head,' I explained once I got home.

'Of course we won't listen to her.'

The phone began ringing violently.

'We won't answer,' said Mum.

'No, course not,' Dad confirmed.

'People like that . . .'

'No, course not.'

'I mean, Kristina, you wouldn't think of . . .'

'What?'

'Doing something . . . like that.'

'No.'

'And you're not telling me a lie?'

'No.'

'Look me in the eyes. Are you lying?'

'No.'

'Is she lying?' asked Dad from behind his paper.

'Doesn't look like it,' Mum conceded.

She looked at Dad. There was tenderness in her eyes, a tenderness with which I nourished myself that evening. Mum and Dad seemed transparent, visions from the canister, from that wonderful world, a world where there were no men and women, no genitals, no wanking, no explosions, no ramming inside the gates of the body, no conception, no pain, no struggle, no walls, no doors, no blinds in front of their eyes. They were humans who reproduced without blood or sperm, reproduced like thoughts, pure and light. They floated inside the canister, forcing me out as the petrol in my brain began to evaporate.

Their faces turned to stone.

On the shelf stood a Matryoshka doll. She was pretty and plump, with chubby, red cheeks and a sly smiling mouth. Dad had brought the Matryoshka from Moscow as a present for Mum, but when Mum didn't stop crying and throwing tantrums the doll wound up in my bedroom. The doll constantly wanted to give birth, and I never tired of helping her. I played midwife whenever her imploring gaze fell on me. I twisted her open and kissed her red lips. Though she diminished in size, she still looked as sly as ever. As I dismantled her, an invisible hand dismantled me.

When I stepped out of the Matryoshka I was small, and practiced different faces in front of the mirror. Mum was sitting near me, her eyes empty, and didn't see when I did the things she had forbidden. My brow furrowed and the corners of my mouth curved downwards. I was Grandma, a bulldog, when Mum suddenly came to and started shouting. I dashed into my room to straighten out my forehead. I stretched the skin with both hands and frowned and hoped that Mum would walk in, and that she wouldn't.

She didn't. A familiar tape was playing inside my head. The tape explained in Mum's voice that I should think about the faces I pulled. I shouldn't forget for a moment what I looked like. I should always smile a little, raising my eyebrows, but I should never frown. It was crucial to differentiate raising your eyebrows from frowning. Frowning was a sin. Raising your eyebrows was a sophisticated gesture that magically made you look happy and gently raised the corners of your mouth. People liked you if you smiled. That's why you *always* had to smile a little. You always had to smile a *little*.

'Even when you're asleep?' I asked.

After a long silence, Mum replied:

'Yes. Then the expression will stay in your subconscious.'

I clenched my eyes shut, tensed every muscle in my face.

'No, Kristina, that's a scowl!' shouted Mum in unison with the tape.

I raised my eyebrows, curved the corners of my mouth up a fraction, and looked Mum right in the eyes. She looked back, her eyebrows raised, her mouth set in a stiff smile. I touched her cheek. It was cold and taut. Her eyes snuffed out. She slumped to the floor and an eye dripping with yellow rheum rolled down on to her cheek.

I tried to hold my smile together with my fingers, but the corners of my mouth wouldn't obey. They twisted themselves back down in spasms, the movement spreading, forcing me to twitch my shoulders and tense my stomach muscles, to shake my hips and jump up and down on the spot, up and down, until the door opened and Pirta walked in.

'What are you doing?'

'Exercise.'

She stood beside me and gave a few lacklustre hops before collapsing on the bed.

'The boys are waiting. Get yourself ready.'

'Kristina, come here a minute,' Mum whispered from the kitchen door. 'Here, take this so you won't frown in front of other folk.'

I swallowed the tablets that she rattled out of a tub decorated on the side with a glossy triangle. My step gradually slowed. By the time I walked across the tracks into Kari's arms I was completely relaxed.

Hands

'I'll mark it here.'

Kari thrust a stick in the ground and wrote: '5th September 1979, Kari and Kristina'. He sucked greedily on his cigarette, and little by little his pupils widened, becoming black mirrors that reflected me, beautiful and multiplied. He grabbed my hand, pushed the squashed cigarette between my lips, and before I could blow the smoke out he stuck his hot tongue into my mouth. The smoke worked its way into my cells, stretching them until I was ready to burst open with love. I kissed him greedily. It was safe to kiss him now, when he was far away, beyond my gaze, far from my swelling breasts and hefty thighs which his hands were gently caressing.

They were strange hands. Throughout the heat of the summer they had grown and strengthened, become hairy and confident. They roamed underneath my clothes and pressed hard, and I didn't even notice the train, as my body was shuddering more violently than the ground and the red-hot tracks.

'Kari and Kristina, you've been spotted!' shouted a track worker and blew his whistle.

We ran along the tracks hand in hand. After we'd crossed the railway bridge we jumped on to the verge and disappeared into the woods for a year, two years, but by evening we were hungry again and Kari's tongue was no longer sweet but bitter, his hands were no longer looking for me but for tobacco, the stuff mixed with marijuana that you could get on the Swedish side if you had the money and the cheek to walk past the customs officers' watchful eyes with your head held high. That's what his hands were looking for in every bag and pocket, but not in me, though I was open and dripping, and I didn't want to close up again so soon.

'Fucking hell, I'll kill myself,' Kari hissed.

It didn't sound exciting any more; it didn't sound like it meant we'd do it together, but that both of us would do it nonetheless, and that it would be for good. It sounded frightening, threatening, intimidating.

'I'll steal some money from my dad,' I whispered.

The hand I held was ice cold. Very slowly it clenched into a fist.

I ran along the tracks to the train station, hid behind a pile of logs and waited for the darkness, which I used to shroud myself as I slipped past our house and across the road to Pirta's place.

'Is your mum at work?'

'Yes, she'll be out all night,' said Pessi.

Pirta's eyes were puffy. Teary mascara had painted lines down her cheeks and her neck. She tried to say something, but burst into tears.

'Aslak's been sleeping around on the Swedish side,' Pessi explained.

I held Pirta tightly, too tightly. Her sobbing crept inside me, only to encounter a boulder that had stood at the mouth of the cave for a long time, far too long. It mustn't move yet. Not now, not here.

'The girls in Sweden have got really big tits!'

'That's enough, you little shit,' screamed Pirta and grabbed Pessi by the hair.

'Let me go or I'll tell Mum!'

'Go ahead, she'll only slap you. Like she did yesterday, and the day before. She hates you,' she snapped as she dragged Pessi into the boiler room.

I followed them and echoed Pirta with a scowl. No sound made it past my tears. They were swelling like a burning pressure in my chest. My eyelids blinked inadvertently and my nose itself twisted into a knot. The boulder was growing, moving up towards my throat. Pessi would be locked in the boiler room, then everything would feel better. The boulder would melt away to nothing; Pessi wouldn't yap on any more.

'Crouch down and start panting,' Pirta ordered.

Pessi slumped to the floor, whimpering.

'Start panting,' she shouted and struck him with her fist.

Pessi spluttered and panted, spluttered and panted. Spit and snot sprayed everywhere. One two three. My voice only just made it past the boulder. It was nothing but a wheeze, a hiss; it wasn't my voice, it wasn't my little brother. Fifteen, a hundred, a hundred and thirty. The boulder began to roll away. Two hundred. Someone bellowed and grabbed my throat.

'Push, for fuck's sake!'

I slumped on top of Pessi and slammed my fists against his chest. Tears flowed into his hair. Pirta leaned against my back, forcing me to push harder, though Pessi was being crushed against the cement floor. She tore off her chiffon scarf and started mopping up the thick blood which flowed in a sticky black stream from the back of Pessi's head.

'Pessi, wake up!' she cried, slapping his white cheeks.

Pessi didn't wake up. From the living room I fetched a woollen shawl and covered him.

'You can't leave now,' Pirta sobbed.

I walked through her; I stepped into the hallway, put on my shoes, and pushed the door open. Heavy snowdrops were falling from the sky. They left a metallic taste on your tongue.

The lights were on in every room in the house. I stood at the kitchen door, blinking frantically. Mum was reorganising her medicine cabinet; she glanced over her shoulder but didn't see me.

'I'll have to start again,' she muttered.

She picked up a box with its own compartment for each day of the week, and began filling it with pills. Dad gave me a smile. My eyes stopped blinking. I looked up at Mum, and when I was sure she wasn't watching, I smiled back at him.

Lynchings

Some people managed to escape, though the village didn't want them to go. Many of them quietly returned and obediently placed themselves back under the microscope. If something in the world had changed, it was quickly redressed. You combed your hair back in front of your eyes, your new clothes were burnt and you dressed in old clothes that smelt of the forest; if your tongue no longer worked properly it was simply cut out. There was nothing quite as dangerous as people jabbering away in a southern accent. Nobody could understand them. They were untrustworthy and proud; they thought only of themselves and not of the village, and at any given moment they would be ready to escape again.

Most people slipped easily back into their old skins, found the marks where their old shoes had pressed into the ground, where it was safe to walk. Nature helped these deserters. The sky drew lower, the forest stretched its limbs closer to the houses and the river sprayed water up on to the road all the time, not just during the spring floods. In small surroundings it's easier to find your old place. The unfortunate events in Kautokeino had taught people that it wasn't advisable to carry out public lynchings all that often, otherwise they would lose their effect.

Back then there had been no town councillor. Where the stone village hall now stood there used to be a manor house. It belonged to Taneli Niva, who was then the village's local police chief. Nothing could change his stubborn mind, though Jesus arrived in the village and with his stick whipped those thirsting to punish him into a religious trance. The result of this was the birth of a new law: everyone had to join the church, kneel before the Lord and beg for the forgiveness of their sins. Taneli refused. Jesus spat in his face and continued on his way to Kautokeino, where he gradually amassed a small army. The men grabbed their shotguns, the women picked up axes and the children were given small sharp knives.

The children's screams woke Taneli just before his door was battered down and the first shot rang out. He had just enough time to slip on his fur boots and stand up and stretch before falling back on his bed and watching from the corner of the ceiling as his body was torn to pieces. His soul managed to escape, but it didn't dare go far. It saw a great golden web, and although it could no longer feel the throttling, it knew that this was to be its place. New brave men were born, and Dad was one of them. He had the courage to oppose the lynchings, and during his time as town councillor only one such lynching had taken place, and that had been at the request of the victim himself.

It was Kalle Piippola, Pekka and Erkki's father. After losing both his sons he got on the train, a noose around his neck, and travelled all the way to the great big city with the great big train station, where he sat in the great hall with other men just like him, nooses around their necks, newspapers crumpled upside down in their laps, their watches stopped, some of them blue in the face. They sat there waiting; every time a new train shook the ground and the doors opened, letting crowds of people flood into the great hall, they stood up, but nobody stopped to look at them and they slumped back to their benches, picked their crumpled newspapers up from the floor – it didn't matter whether it was that day's paper, last week's, last year's – and read until their eyeballs were awash with printer's ink. Announcements echoed around the great hall; they echoed endlessly. Trains came in at different times, arrived at different platforms. They shook the hard benches so much that Kalle could no longer hear his own heartbeat. He ran out to the platform, got on the train that had brought both his sons south, and began his journey back to the village. The noose around his neck loosened. He could breathe again and dared to believe that his sons would be waiting for him at the train station in the village, that they would be waiting for their father as he had waited in vain for them.

But the village station was empty, so empty that the train didn't even stop. It just slowed down slightly, allowing Kalle to jump out at speed, and before evening fell he was hanging lifeless from the gates of the village hall. He hadn't needed much help. He climbed up the ladder and tied the rope by himself. Dad gave him a helping hand by prodding his legs with a broom. After Kalle died, Dad claimed he hadn't prodded him at all, but there had been lots of witnesses. They gathered in front of the village hall expecting Dad to give a speech. They wanted to hear that no one should follow Kalle's example.

Dad tried to defend himself, though nobody was accusing him of anything. The men in the family all had that same stubborn spirit. Dad waved the broom in the air and swore that he had never used it to hit anyone, though everyone had seen him use it to swipe the backsides of the drunks congregating in the doorway outside the village hall. In the paper there was a picture of Dad running after the Indians with his broom when they had surrounded him and were making their demands. Nobody blamed Dad for that either. Somebody had to keep order. If there was no common language, you had to use the broom; it was a language everybody understood. Best of all I understood Doughnut, on whose lips such accusations turned to a soft whimpering. It felt safe to keep these accusations to yourself, savour them and swallow them bit by bit until your stomach was full.

Pessi

The days felt clammy and safe. Then a couple of social workers turned up at Pirta and Pessi's house.

'Mum's at work,' Pirta informed them.

The women walked past her and into the living room where Pessi was kneeling in front of the television, his bruised nose buried deep in a swab of cotton wool doused in thinner. A half-finished roll-up lay smouldering in the ashtray.

'Is that marijuana?' asked one of the women.

'No, it's *The Exorcist II*,' Pessi replied.

Pessi left with the women and Pirta finished her cigarette. The girl on the television changed shape as the forces of evil ravaged her body.

The days felt clammy and safe, and whistles shrieked inside me. My cheeks were still plump and my stomach bulged unless I held it in all the time. I hadn't reached my target. I still couldn't pull on the jeans I had worn when I was ten. I still had to go to the toilet, even though I made myself throw up after every meal. If there was food in my stomach I couldn't concentrate on my homework or go out with my friends.

I had become transparent. I no longer had to play Fainting or ask Pirta to press her hands against my chest. I fainted getting out of bed in the morning and my dreams carried me far away. When I looked in the mirror I couldn't see my body; the fat had disappeared from around the faint aura of my reflection. I couldn't see my spasms. In the dusk my body gave off a dim yellow light, but apart from this the image I saw was dominated by my eyes, which had grown to the size of the mirror and had become a spring. Above the spring the leaves turned yellow and floated down to the surface of my icy hymen, then down to the frozen ground where the wind swept them away. Nature waited for a moment, bare and unharnessed, grieving for the summer that had passed. Then snow fell, wonderful white snow. It warmed the trees' naked bodies and illuminated a world which was shattered each night by the cry of the passing train.

They were on their way, the figures cloaked in black. My dreams were transparent too, like bones revealed beneath the layers of fat. They floated through my room in the daytime too, even when I was awake.

House arrest

I stiffened when I saw their new seating arrangement. They were intertwined.

Dad's hand was resting on Mum's shoulder. Mum's leg was on top of Dad's thigh. When they saw me they put down their shot glasses and burst into tears.

'Mum, has someone died?'

'Yes, yes,' she spluttered.

'Our trust has died,' Dad informed me.

'You've been seen.'

'Behind the tracks.'

'Smooching.'

'And as for that swine.'

'He's a bastard child.'

'A cleaner's brat.'

'The shame.'

'The terrible, terrible shame.'

Their voices overlapped. They became one. Then Mum suddenly broke away screaming. She had clenched her glass in her hand so hard that it had smashed. Blood was running from her fingers.

'Hang around with him again and I'll kill you.'

'She will, you know,' Dad said.

I was grounded for a week. I lay under a pile of thick blankets and took my temperature until it had finally risen. The nights were already below freezing. I grieved for Kari, who was measuring the height of the platform, his fingers numb, and who thought I'd abandoned him. When the train approached I got out of bed and opened the window. Uncontrolled spasms froze on my face. My mouth was unable to pout, my nose didn't twitch, but my body still writhed. I removed my flannel nightie, climbed out of the window and rested on the roof ladder. There I lay in the pale moonlight, listening to the crackling as my limbs froze stiff.

I would die as the train swept across the rail bridge up towards the darkening sky. I would die there, my lungs full of Kari's warm breath. I wouldn't die now, not just yet, even though the church bells clanged and the pale moonlight became hot and searing and heavy eyelids slowly darkened the world. Their inner surface was a sweltering forest in which cigarettes lit up by themselves and spring water boiled in whirlpools. Kari placed his fingers on my neck, brushed my spine into view and hid away the fat, and I was happy and thin. Never again would he say:

'Fucking hell, Kristina, you've got big thighs.'

On the other side of my eyelids was morning, creeping in through Nan's windows, beckoning me outside to smell the awakening forest, to measure the earth's steady pulse with my feet. I walked through a small woodland and came to a field with hay growing, quietly reaching up towards the sky; slender stalks yielding food for the reindeer does and their small calves standing beside them staring, their antlers bold and proud upon their heads.

I bravely carried on towards the shore, even though a reindeer stag stood at the edge of the woods, as dignified as a statue, its nostrils wide and quivering. It was autumn and the reindeer were afflicted by a madness. I walked, drawn towards the stag, keeping my eyes fixed on the lake where I was about to take a dip. The reindeer's velvety antlers rattled. Thick hair grew on my palms. A white calf nudged me with its antlers. I fell on my hands and knees and let my head droop beneath me, my lips touching the ground.

'I won't kill you. It's myself I'm going to kill.'

I listened to his voice. Words didn't mean anything. He asked me why I hadn't told him my secrets. Why hadn't I reached out my hand as we were walking along the village road? Why had I locked my bedroom door and refused to open up, even after he'd asked me nicely? Why hadn't I opened the door, even though he had cried and begged me?

Between those words ran a quiet path; I crept along it and into his arms.

I was inside him. He enveloped me like a grey mist, a blend of colours, dim blue, golden yellow. Grandma walked in, Mum stirred and the grey dispersed. Mum's lips rounded into a smile. Inside Grandma she calmly breathed in. Inside Mum I calmly breathed out. When Grandma disappeared I fell once again into the dampness of the bed.

'It's because of your father, you know, not because of you,' Mum whispered.

I touched my face, ran my fingers along the bony rims of my eye sockets. My body had lost its shape. Bones had dissolved into dust. I was great, immense. Mum's gaunt face, her mouth repeating silent words. Small and tepid. In a gentle stream she flowed through the house's fragile walls.

Death

The Matryoshka had a boyfriend, a doll carved of wood with a frozen face and piercing eyes. It looked more like a statue than a doll, but it was more expressive than anyone in the house. I placed it at the foot of the bed and looked at it in the dark each night before going to bed and after waking up each morning.

The doll had endless different expressions. Dad said it was meant to represent Padmasambhava, the man who long ago had brought a new religion to Tibet. Looking at the doll, my face relaxed and I was able to step out of my protective armour. I often spent entire days staring at it. As I looked at the doll, my every last thought disappeared.

I glided inside Mum and rested in her carefully guarded cave. She let me in. She hadn't built a stone wall to keep me out, a fortress within which she appeared soft and generous. Her face shimmered through the dimness inside.

Mum was in constant motion.

In my dream cave a ruddy face pierced the wooden doll's frozen expression. The two shifted back and forth until the soft face was around the outside and the hard face propped like a stake in the middle.

Mum was sitting at the piano, her face moving with the music, until the sound of the piano disappeared and was replaced by that of a twanging sitar that bent Mum's fingers and refracted her body's rainbow into a dazzling spectrum of colours. The Mum I knew was like a little doll at the centre of this motion. I spoke to her in my wooden doll's language and she replied in her own. I shook my infinite bodies and the house straightened its spine, making it safe to sit there protected by porous layers of bark.

When Grandma died, I lay the Tibetan doll in her cold arms.

Mum fed Dad with Diazepam.

'And don't you be blubbing in front of other folk,' she instructed him.

One glance at the doll, however, and she changed her mind.

'Blub if you like.'

Mum sewed Grandma some white clothes. Dad made a coffin, and the evening before the funeral Grandma was laid on the porch outside. We sat in the living room crying and hugging one another. The television was shrouded in a white cloth and on top of that was a candle which illuminated the translucent figures behind the window as they huddled around Grandma's coffin.

At the graveside a shovel was passed from hand to hand. Misted wreaths warmed the air and sobs collected in frost flowers on the wooden cross. Mum started wailing as her temples burst open. Her uterus had closed shut, so she couldn't be reborn with Grandma on the other side.

She would have to stay in the house.

Sports hall

'Have you put on weight again?' Kari asked.

'Maybe. Don't come any closer.'

'I won't,' he retorted and walked up into the stands.

The walls of the sports hall were trembling. The floor was awash with kissing couples and drunken teenagers. Volunteers from the church knelt next to the people who had passed out and measured their pulses. I looked down wistfully at the long-jump pit. The last time I had been here, when Dingo had been performing, I'd lain there beneath Kari and my trousers had become filled with sand. A pain shot through the bottom of my stomach as I remembered his touch.

Now Kari was standing up on the podium, hugging a strange girl.

Birgitta was standing in the doorway.

'Where are you going, Kristina?'

'Inside.'

'Heaven or Hell?'

'Inside.'

I held out the banknote I'd stolen from Dad. The assistant pressed a tingling stamp into the back of my hand.

'Wash it off, Kristina. It's the mark of the Devil!' Birgitta shouted after me.

I was already on my way into the hall, at the centre of which the lead singer stood on a brightly lit stage singing and rubbing his leopardskin-clad genitals. There was nothing for it but to take off my jacket and start dancing, to stare insistently at his crotch as my dry lips tried to catch the words raining from his mouth.

Buns snug in the oven, the dough's a-rising, baby let's get cooking, he crooned.

The air was thick; the hall was crammed full with figures gyrating in time with the music. People sat hugging and kissing on the benches lining the walls. I sat down on a bench and waited for my breath to even out.

'Fucking hell, Angela, you've got big thighs.'

The girl giggled. Kari's face lit up. The clock ticked onwards. Finally the hall's glaring lights were switched on.

I walked along a pavement lined with faint streetlights. Cars slowed down, their doors opened. I could feel their pull; my lips were moist with drink, my pores wide open with longing. I shook my head and they continued on their way.

Dad came back in the early hours, cracked open a bottle of beer and collapsed in front of the television. I washed up a bowl and baked another tiger cake, then a chocolate cake, then a spiced cake, then gingerbread biscuits. As I took the seventh tray of biscuits out of the oven, Dad switched off the television and went out again. I washed up the dishes and wiped the table, scrubbed the tiles and wiped down the cooker top. I took a broom and swept the floor. Crumbs stuck revoltingly in between the bristles.

Doughnut's howling was momentarily drowned out by the hum of the vacuum cleaner.

I was in the sauna filling a bucket of water when I heard the garage door rattle. I peered out of the sauna window into the yard and saw Dad striding along the moonlit path outside. He threw the padlock to the floor. Pirta's mum was running towards him with her arms outstretched.

The water splashed gaily as I sloshed the mop about in the bucket. The floor was very dirty indeed! I changed the water and mopped the floor a second time. When the clock chimed five times I decided perhaps I had done enough cleaning for one day. Only the breakfast table remained. I laid the cups out neatly and carefully folded the floral napkins. After putting the porridge oats in water to soak, I went to the bathroom.

There was a sticky film across my teeth. I brushed my teeth for a long time and went into the shower. I spread soap over my skin and scrubbed myself with a brush, but the smell of cake wouldn't go away. It soaked deep into my skin and took on a shape all of its own. My stomach filled up, but I couldn't make myself sick. I couldn't get to sleep either as, with my skin stinging, I finally lay down in my clean bed.

Dad had broken his promise. The mercury dropped from minus thirty to minus forty. Doughnut stopped howling.

Interrogation

A long corridor ran from the toilets down to the refectory. The corridor glistened with sneering faces and mouths blackened with gossip. As she saw me, Pirta turned to face the wall and stuck out her behind. I shook my fringe to one side and walked past her into the refectory.

Hips clothed in an apron swung back and forth on the other side of the hatch. I selected a plate that was filled to the edges, covered my crispbread with thick, creamy slices of cheese, and looked for a corner where I could sit with my back to those who had ganged up against me. The comforting stodge gently slid down my gullet. My stomach expanded; I lifted up my jumper and secretly undid my top trouser button. My stomach swelled into a protective ball. Mocking glances bumped softly against it and bounced back to their senders.

Only once I was at the door of the refectory, as the desolation of the entrance hall made me tense my stomach muscles, was my diaphragm consumed by an itch that my fingers desperately wanted to scratch off. I staggered along the corridor past Pirta's arse, past the scornful eyes, the gossiping mouths, past the legs trying to trip me up, all the way to the toilets, which dutifully opened their door and shut me inside one of the small, stinking cubicles. I stuck my fingers down my throat and gagged until my stomach was empty and had shrunk back into a small ball.

I rinsed my face, dried it on the edge of my jumper and stepped into the smoking circle.

'Don't say a word to anyone, okay?' Pirta hissed and moved to one side.

Smoke hid the anger. For a moment we were one again. We could sense the approaching teaching assistant and threw the cigarette end down the toilet just before the door opened.

'Who was it? Own up!'

I took a Danish pastry out of my pocket and stuffed it into my mouth. Five hundred calories. I jogged back home through the village and stopped at the gate to catch my breath. Pirta's mum came to the door and shouted:

'On you go inside, Kristina. The police have already left.'

'You should be ashamed of yourself!' shouted Mum. 'We'll never live this down, and your father'll lose his job!'

I sat down on the edge of an armchair. Mum and Dad sat on the sofa looking at me.

'Were you involved?' asked Mum.

'No.'

'You do know what I'm talking about.'

'No.'

'Are you fooling about?'

'No.'

'I'm talking about . . . about . . .'

Mum burst into tears. Dad cleared his throat and loosened his shirt collar.

'Well. You've been teasing Pessi . . . beaten him up. His head was bleeding.'

'Did you do it? Answer me!' Mum screamed.

'No.'

'Who did it then? Pirta?'

'It wasn't me.'

'Kristina, for the last time. Were you involved?'

'No.'

'Kristina, look me in the eyes.'

I moved my fringe to one side. Green water was dripping from Mum's eyes.

'Would you lie to your own mother?'

'No.'

'So you didn't do it? Did you do it? Didn't you?'

'No.'

'Would you even think of doing something like that?'

'No.'

Dad leapt up and yanked the tie from around his neck.

'Speak properly!' he bellowed.

'No no no.'

'Kristina. If you're lying to us, you know very well what'll happen. We'll lose our trust, and if we haven't got that we'll have nothing. Everything will disappear. Our lives will be ruined. All our lives.'

'They're already ruined,' Mum whispered, staring at the bruises on Dad's neck.

'Trust . . .' Dad began once again.

'Don't you listen to your father, Kristina. Don't listen to him.'

Mum's words became long and unclear. A yellowish

foam appeared at the corners of her mouth. I walked her into the bedroom and tucked her into bed. Then I ran outside and pulled Doughnut from his kennel. Dad ran away from us across the street. Doughnut and I ran through the woods and along the paths through the village. He lagged behind, his tongue trailing the ground, and quickly marked his territory. My legs refused to stop. Five hundred calories. Mum was sitting at the table sobbing when I got back from my jog. I loaded a tray full of food and disappeared into my room with Doughnut.

While Doughnut devoured the food I did press-ups on the floor until I collapsed on my face and the ceiling caved in. Five hundred calories. I lifted the house back upright and put on my aerobics cassette. I jumped up and down and spun around until Mum knocked on the door, smiling a stiff, rediscovered smile. I smiled back, because smiling was a movement just like any other, and it burned calories too. At the dinner table I stuffed the sandwich Mum gave me into my mouth and started chewing. Fifty times, a hundred, a hundred and fifty.

'Good to see you chewing properly, lass. Digestion starts in your mouth,' she said.

She was sitting on a kitchen stool with Dad's trousers in her lap.

'You're both sick,' Dad shouted.

Then he ran outside.

Kennel

Steam filled my nostrils and stopped me from breathing. I got up from the table, but Mum's glare pushed me back into my chair. I put the lid back on the pot and Mum took it off again.

'Stop playing with your food.'

Steam rose up again. It could still rise into the air, even though it was heavy with different smells. Meat, pepper, potatoes. These smells stuck to me, burrowed deep inside me and turned to fat. I held out my plate. Mum ladled it full of soup. I poured the soup back into the pot. Mum stuck the ladle into the soup. I held my hands over my plate and shook my head. Mum poured the soup over my hands. Boiling hot, thick soup.

'It's the end of the world,' Dad wept.

'She burnt my hands,' I wept.

'She won't eat anything, just stares into space,' Mum wept.

'That mutt's dribbling on the floor again,' Dad pointed out. 'Should be put down.'

'Get to your kennel,' Mum screamed.

Kari would come and saw through the bars. He'd shoot Mum and Dad. He'd lift me into his arms and carry me out into the freezing cold, let me hold him tight round the waist as we rode together on the scooter. He'd pull up outside the cottage once the fire had gone out, once the coals glowed in a sea of orange that lit the room and warmed us.

Kari would come. The train's cry filled the kennel, almost like a promise. Kari would come before dawn. Then morning would come again, once the sun had finally dared to pass over the long border of darkness.

Urho

The fat melted away and I neared my target. A small pile of bones would be all that was left of me when I took my final breath and flew far away to continue my life in another form, perhaps on a different planet. I was still breathing faintly, but there was clearly some space between me and the pile of bones. By sheer force of will I remained invisible and managed to avoid the taunts of Pirta and her new gang. During class I soaked up knowledge. During break I went through my homework. I didn't have to revise for exams, because the pages became imprinted on my mind after a single glance. In exams I copied material from the smooth cloth of my mind and got straight As.

Sometimes, very rarely, I got an A minus. Mum started paying attention.

'What happened? Didn't you double-check?'

She scoffed when I told her that my mistakes were caused by the macaroni she had insisted that I eat before leaving for school. You needed an empty stomach to achieve perfection. There should be nothing but stomach acids in there. A carrot eaten the day before and not thrown up was enough to disturb your concentration. Little by little this became a great ink stain on my mind's cloth, spreading out, slowly obscuring the letters and numbers.

Mum was in the bedroom sighing. Dad had returned home and was doing his laundry. He held wet clothes up to the light and crammed them back into the machine.

'They won't clean,' he complained. 'They just won't.'

'It'll be the end of the world,' Mum agreed.

She looked at Urho, who had turned up uninvited, and gave him a tight smile.

'The fallout will be here soon enough if the wind changes,' he explained.

'It's a while since the last time.'

'Thirteen years, just before Kristina was born.'

'You never know what'll happen. The sickness is there inside.'

'What year was it the reindeer had calves with no eyes?'

'It was the year Kristina was born.'

I stood at the window. The snowfall thickened and the flakes changed colour. They were pink. Urho turned his eyes on me; they sparkled like bright little lamps.

'You've not been to the library for a while now, Kristina.'

Snow pushed through the glass.

'Kristina reads at home these days,' Dad said.

'Is that right? And what do you read?'

'School books.'

'School books?'

'Aye, Kristina's concentrating on her school,' Dad said.

'School books,' repeated Urho in disgust.

Dad asked whether it was dangerous to eat berries and mushrooms, as they too might contain large amounts of radioactive iodine. In response, Urho turned his cup upside down and stomped out into the hallway.

'School books, for crying out loud,' he muttered.

The snow mapped his footprints. I hopped along them all the way to the village hall. Growth rings fell on to the snow around me like the folds of a gypsy skirt. I was small and light as I stepped into the large, open room where Dad greeted me happily from his seat amongst his piles of papers. I left my outdoor clothes in his office and bounded up the stairs to the library. I wandered between the shelves in the adults' section, pulled the most interesting books from their neat rows and disappeared back to the children's section where I hid the books behind copies of Donald Duck.

I was used to reading in secret, I didn't know any other way, though Urho could see through me. His mind was like a cloudless sky which, unable to remain hidden beneath his scalp, floated in the air above me as I sat reading and studying. Each week new books appeared on the shelves, as if to complement the knowledge I had absorbed the last time I had sat reading in the cartoon corner.

We didn't speak often. His eyes would tell me if there was anything interesting for me on the shelves. If there was nothing new, he would wink at me and allow me to immerse myself in an old book whose yellowed pages came loose as I excitedly flicked through them in search of the story of Bhaisajyaraja and the Buddha named Sun and Moon Glow. If Urho was working by himself he would let me sit by the fireplace, stoke the fire and leave me in peace.

Bhaisajyaraja's fontanelle never closed over. His spiritual endeavours reaped great reward. He fervently worshipped his teacher Buddha Sun and Moon Glow, and as a gesture of his devotion he resolved to sacrifice his own body.

He drank litres of fragrant oils and doused his cloak in them, then set himself on fire. There he burned like a torch for twelve thousand years. Eventually he died, was reborn and reunited with Buddha Sun and Moon Glow, who was still alive. He then followed his teacher until he finally passed away.

To house his teacher's relics, Bhaisajyaraja erected eighty-four thousand stupas and oversaw the funeral ceremony himself. At the end of the ceremony he set light to both his arms. They burned in honour of Buddha Sun and Moon Glow for seventy-two thousand years.

I stuck my hands into the flames, only to pull them out again quickly with a squeal. The hairs had been singed and gave off a sharp stench. The skin was slightly red. I was angry at another one of the monks I had just read about. After setting himself alight he just sat there with his legs crossed, smiling.

He smiled until his body shrivelled up and turned to ashes. His smile floated above the place he had been sitting, and years later a golden temple was built there to mark the spot.

I didn't take home the books which I most longed for. Urho made up piles of books for me to take home, each containing a mix of youth culture and adult classics. From the library I went down to Dad's office and started reading until the pile became smaller. Getting started was difficult because, far away from Urho, black clouds began gathering in the sky, forcing me to count the number of lines in the books. A quick count wasn't enough. I knew I could read through five lines at a glance, and at the end of the page it was easy to times the number of glances by five. Sometimes I got caught up in the story and forgot to count. I would read for hours at a time, sometimes for entire days, and didn't once raise my eyes from the book, though at times the text would escape from my eyes and disappear into a deep ravine. I would hold my breath as I read. Sometimes my concentration would wander and I would see how many pages I could read without taking a breath.

Dad flicked through his papers and chuckled as I gasped for breath. I only stopped when the door opened and one of the staff walked in.

'She's a clever lass,' said the intruder.

'Kristina's moved up to the adults' section now,' said Dad proudly.

'Years ago, actually,' I muttered and screwed up my eyes.

'Show us here,' Dad said.

'Russian?'

'Aye. Kristina likes Chekhov's use of language and the suspended sense of atmosphere.'

Once the intruder had left Dad gave me a kiss and ruffled my hair.

'You and me, Kristina. We're geniuses.'

'You and me, Kristina,' said Mum as she dragged me from the window and stood me in front of the mirror. 'Just like me and Grandma. It sticks out.'

My pelvis protruded through the mirror. I stepped through the mirror and walked out to the edge of a cliff where Alina sat, her legs dangling down into the ravine.

'You and me, Kristina,' she said tragically.

'Alina, don't jump!'

She attached two balls of wax to her head and lit a match.

'Hold your back straight!' Mum shouted from behind the mirror.

Alina's hair was ablaze. When I turned back to face Mum, she fell.

Passenger train

The passenger train arrived. Pirta had known about this since the summer. It came up from the south once a week, stopped in the village, continued north to Kolari, then stopped in the village on its way back the following day.

A passenger train full of good-looking boys. All you had to do was wait. And wait. And wait.

'I'll be ready and waiting!' Pirta declared.

But no boys ever turned up. An old couple arrived from Aavasaksa, and someone who lived in the village but had been visiting family. Sometimes the only person to get off the train was the conductor, who glanced up and down the empty platform and got back on the train blowing his nasty whistle. The sound penetrated my eardrum and reminded me that I would have to come back the following night, the following week. Whenever the train passed through, I had to be there, because Kari would be there measuring the tracks and taking notes. Checking the clock was Angela, the girl with short, backcombed hair, skinny as a rake.

Angela was better than me. Angela lived in Naistenkangas on the Swedish side where, as a child, Mum had worked herding the cows. They were wonderful summers. The men had been over on the Finnish side building houses. Grandpa only showed up every now and then, and Grandma hadn't always remembered to ruffle Mum's hair. Only in the autumn did a small bald patch appear that was easy to cover with a cap.

Angela didn't wear a cap. She pretended to be cocky and walked around with her nose in the air. I walked around with my eyes fixed on the ground and didn't pretend to be anything, but Angela was still better. Kari had told Pirta that Angela had better tits and that at least she didn't screw her face up all the time. He had told Pirta because he didn't want to see me any more. He didn't know that the layers of fat hid my spasms from view. They had disappeared beneath my skin, back beneath the slimy surface of my organs. They had immersed themselves in my spinal fluids and formed their own writhing community, their own little hell that shot messages up to my brain:

'Go to the station!'

There was no resisting that command. Even in the middle of the night I would get up, pull Dad's lambskin coat over me to warm my bones, hide behind the piles of logs and stare out into the woods, watching Pirta's runaway father, his eyes flashing through the darkness, shouting commands at the wolves. I had to crawl closer, let them attack me, maul me, rip open my thin hide and gnaw on my heavy, broken bones.

The front door opened. Birgitta came in with the cold.

'Shut the door, quickly!' Mum shouted.

'Kristina might like to take a break, take some time off school,' said Birgitta.

'No,' Mum replied.

'No,' I replied when Mum handed me the bread basket. 'I won't eat if I can't eat by myself. If I can't eat by myself, I won't go to school.'

Mum closed her eyes. A minus, B plus, C, D minus, fail, destruction, destruction, destruction.

Cold rampaged through the living room. Mum hit it over the head with a ladle and rushed to close the door behind Birgitta. Heavy steam rose from the plate as I carried it into my room. Doughnut followed me, his nostrils quivering, though he found it difficult to get up the stairs because he was so overweight. My face turned as I swallowed my laxative tablets. My empty bowel convulsed trying to force out the mucus and the air. Rough sand scratched the twists of my gut. It wouldn't come out, though I washed the pills down with a bucketful of water. Thoughts accumulated in my bowels. They would disappear when I moved, but because I was so underweight my body no longer obeyed me. My legs didn't want to run. They carried me slowly along the frozen path, and not even the cold would burn calories for me any longer.

Time stumbled along in front of me. I couldn't keep up with Uncle as he marched towards the frozen villages by the lakes. Sometimes he would slow his pace and let me shuffle in front of him.

'Kristina, what day did the ice break up in 1900?'

'Kristina, what day of the week I was born?'

'Kristina, how many kilometres have we walked?'

'Kristina, how many minutes have you been alive?'

'Kristina, how many calories have you burned in your life?'

I didn't have the energy to talk and so he answered himself. He picked me up a few times and held me in his arms. His unwashed skin smelled of death. He carried me until I had the strength to drag myself onwards.

Mum was lying in bed. Dad was at meetings every evening. I trundled from one room to another; sometimes I trundled to school, where I sat by myself in the corner of an echoing hall or cowered by the radiator in the toilets. Those in the smoking circle moved closer together whenever I looked at them. Pirta walked right through me.

At the weekend I trundled over to the sports hall and sat down in the heated doorway, where Birgitta stared at me with burning coals in her eyes.

'Do you want to commit your life to Jesus Christ?'

'No.'

The floor shook and the walls sloped towards me. I ran out into the yard which was full of cars, their windscreens steamed up with desire.

'Kristina, come over here!' Kari shouted.

'No.'

'Have a drink!' Pirta sneered.

I walked through the car park with their Lada at my heels. The window opened again.

'You're a fair sight!'

The cold had made Pirta's nipples hard. Stuffy air wafted out of the car and warmed me for a moment. They drove off. I took off my mittens and stepped out on to the ice. Stars rained through the palms of my hands and fell to the ground. Inside the heavy lambskin coat my bones boomed with the cold. My fingers dropped off one by one and landed on the rock-hard snowdrifts. My breath was invisible, though the frozen air was dry and overwhelming. Part of me was still in my body as it slowly trudged across the hardened crust, my legs every now and then sinking through into the deep, rough snow. The house loomed at the top of the riverbank like a deserted castle, like my abandoned body.

The lights went on as I walked into the house. From all directions I returned to my core, to the space that was too small for me.

Dad lay curled on the sofa, his eyes fixed on the black screen.

Mum was kneeling on the floor.

And on the floor were her pills, rolling towards the cellar as the house attempted to turn on its side.

'The shame of it. Alina set fire to herself in our cottage.'

All night I followed the movement of the mercury as the cold tightened its grip. The indicator moved downwards and stopped at minus fifty. The mist behind my forehead reluctantly gave way to the blue light of morning. There was no point in waiting for the sun. It wouldn't show its face in the village for a long time yet.

Eventually the cold relented and fresh snow fell – pure, white snow to cover the red. I slowly walked along the railway tracks as the fluids within my body froze solid. Pirta was huddling at the side of the station cabin, her hair white with frost.

'Don't say anything,' she pleaded.

The cold stiffened around my neck. From Pirta's eyelashes dangled little icicles which her tears tried in vain to melt. I opened my coat and held her against me.

'You're like a skeleton,' she whispered.

'Thanks a lot.'

'Nobody came,' she sobbed as we staggered down to the railings.

The tracks began to howl and a train shot out of the black chasm. I pushed Pirta off the railing and ran towards the platform.

'An extra train!' Kari shouted.

The door opened and the conductor hopped out on to the ground.

'Pello. Half an hour,' he announced.

'Great,' we whispered in unison.

All the train doors opened.

Refugees

The refugees were brought in by train. They were housed in draughty outhouses belonging an old skiing centre. It seemed that none of them wanted to show their faces. The men all had long black beards. The women wore veils in front of their faces, some of them had covered their eyes with a tightly woven net. Their bodies too were cloaked in swathes of black cloth.

Dad thought it was a shame.

The whole village thought it was a shame that the newcomers chose to conceal themselves. They couldn't be trusted. The fact that they might have been tortured in their own countries was no reason for them to barge into our village only to hide away. In fact, none of them ever actually claimed to have been tortured. The fact that nobody spoke their language was just an excuse.

Dad changed after the arrival of the refugees. He dressed more smartly, selected his own clothes each morning and didn't take any notice of Mum's advice. He eagerly took care of the refugees' needs: employed a cleaner to visit the camp, as they seemed unable to sort this out amongst themselves and one of them repeatedly defecated on the floor. He organised a collection of old clothes, so that the refugees wouldn't freeze in their draughty outhouses.

One evening as he came back from the camp, his cheeks aglow, he told us that the women had given up their cloaks and dressed in the donated furs and woolly clothes.

Mum was suddenly interested in what Dad had learned through the interpreter.

He had learned that young Abdullah resembled an old man after spending two years confined in a darkened cell.

He learned that Old Hossam had once been treated by a doctor who specialised in the medicine of torture.

He learned that Mustafa's heel had been smashed to pieces and that it would never get better.

'It'll ache forever,' Mum lamented.

'And the boy's only fourteen,' he added.

'The same age as our Kristina, God help us!'

I ran across the ice to the camp. During the day the temperature had risen above freezing and the snow on the ice was soft, but it carried me because my body was weightless. Nobody stopped me as I walked around all the outhouses looking for the boy who was just as sick as I was. I was one of them and they smiled at me. They didn't ask why I was so thin, so transparent.

Mustafa was in a tent with a heater. He was barefoot. A thick bandage had been tied around one of his heels.

I stepped towards him. He reached out his arms, looked upwards and started spinning around. He stamped wildly on the ground, and when he raised his hands grass began to grow. I searched for his eyes and discarded my own. First the fur coat fell from around me, then my skin. I danced around my bones until he suddenly stopped still, and then I knew it was time to rise up and spread my wings.

I flew far away. Flying was easy. The numbness was gone and the forest where I landed blossomed into life. The reindeer does with plump bellies stumbled through the parched woodland and stared at me with great round eyes as I hovered above the spring, looking in vain for my reflection.

I wasn't in the forest. I was on a journey towards the light, and just as I was about to melt away, a helicopter arrived.

River

I was gassed into unconsciousness. My blood vessels burst open. Cloudy solutions flowed through tubes and into my body as it lay on a bed slowly swelling up. I floated in the no-man's-land between breathing in and breathing out. I hung suspended in the limbo between life and death, trying to tell the good sounds from the bad ones. I learned to accept the brightening lights, and I was about to merge with them when Kari took me by the hand.

'Fucking hell, Kristina, not yet!'

When I finally returned to my body the tubes had been disconnected and Christmas carols were blaring through the loudspeakers. I found myself feasting on roast Christmas ham and mashed swede.

Dad guided me into the house.

'It was anorexia nervosa,' he insisted.

'No, it was a very long Ramadan,' I said.

There was a new smell in the hallway. Mum was lying in bed in her silk pyjamas. Her nails were clipped. She smiled as her soft fingers touched my hand.

'And who are you?' she asked.

'Your mother's finally lost it,' Dad explained.

'Aye, that's right, completely lost it,' Mum agreed.

Dad fetched a tray from the kitchen. 'Spruce tea. To improve your appetite.'

We slurped our tea in silence. The whole house was filled with the dim glow of a midwinter's day. Mum's smile opened the living room window and snowflakes drifted inside.

'It's so white,' she whispered.

The river was still covered in wisps of pink mist. The ice crackled and boomed as I ran to the other side. The chanting from the tent melted the fat bulging around my waist and breasts. The aura grew and illuminated the village, bathing it in half-light while the train station remained shrouded in black shadows.

On the crusted snow the light turned blue.

They found Uncle in a snowdrift. His limbs were stiff and straight when they forced him into the coffin. Grandma's resting place had already been breached. She shivered with cold as they laid Uncle's heavy body down upon her fragile bones. In the photograph placed next to a candle in remembrance she was holding a younger Uncle by the hand and smiling warmly.

'Have more food,' she said.

I went round the table for the seventh time. Fried reindeer meat floated in fat; it had already congealed, but once it reached my stomach it quickly melted, mixed with the fat I had already swallowed, and started to boil. I cooled my stomach with ice cream; I pushed every second spoonful into Mum's mouth. She groaned with pleasure, swallowed and licked her lips. Snow worms wriggled their way from Mum's mouth to the spoon and from the spoon into my mouth. The worms ate up the food inside me, and I had to go round the table again so that hunger wouldn't knock me unconscious.

From the rectory we drove to Ruuhijärvi. Mum was left in the living room and tied to the arms of the chair. People carried cakes and booze to the table. I withdrew into Uncle's old room and curled up on top of the dog hairs on the bed. Drunken voices slithered in beneath the door. Every now and then the door opened and sickly breath disturbed the dog hairs.

'Come out here with us, Kristina.'

I curled into an even tighter ball. The worms were squashed and started frantically eating everything in my stomach. I staggered towards the cakes and the noise, but thick walls grew in front of me and I couldn't get past them.

'Come, come,' said another uncle, alive and plump.

His chubby fingers reached out towards me. I went back into the bedroom and curled up tighter and tighter so as not to feel the hunger. My hands pressed deep into my stomach. Pure and clear, the river flowed through a lush green landscape.

'You and me, Kristina,' it said, and swallowed me whole.

Kari was diving in the water's cool undercurrent. When I came to the surface and floated on my back, I could see his hands dangling from a cloud.

'Fucking hell, Kristina, I'm hungry. I could eat a horse!' he yelled.

I swam ashore with long strokes. Far off the train cried out. Kari was standing on the riverbank; his lips were moving, but his voice couldn't be heard above the train.

Light

The conductor blew his whistle. The people in black cloaks were transferred to Kiiruna.

All that was left was the light.

Mum was made redundant and no longer had access to the hospital's medicine stores. Her own medicine cabinet grew steadily emptier. The light grew brighter. Mum pulled up the blinds. Nobody gave her any new medication. She recovered.

Dad washed the windows and light filled the house. As the train careered through my head he was standing in the hallway giving Mum a kiss.

While they were kissing I emptied Dad's wallet of its banknotes. I packed a bag with a few changes of clothes and a book that Urho had given me the last time I'd been to the library.

I waited behind a pile of logs for the train and read, my fingers numb with the cold.

I read about a man who stopped eating and who was

cured of all his ailments. Like a plant he lived on water and light.

The train pulled into the station. I climbed aboard and began heading south.